GONE NORTH

Charles Alden Seltzer

GONE NORTH

CHARLES ALDEN SELTZER

COVER BY

PAUL STAHR

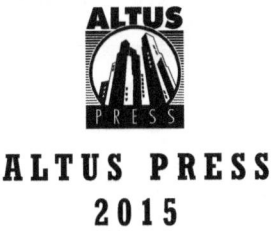

ALTUS PRESS
2015

© 2015 Steeger Properties, LLC, under license to Altus Press • First Edition—2015

EDITED AND DESIGNED BY
Matthew Moring

PUBLISHING HISTORY
"Gone North" originally appeared in the March 22, 29, April 5, 12, 19, and 26, 1930 issues of *Argosy* magazine (Vol. 211 No. 1–Vol. 211 No. 6). Copyright © 1930 by The Frank A. Munsey Company. Copyright renewed © 1957 and assigned to Steeger Properties, LLC. All rights reserved.

THANKS TO
Chad Calkins, Joel Frieman & Chris Kalb

ISBN
978-1-61827-187-7

Visit *altuspress.com* for more books like this.
Printed in the United States of America.

TABLE OF CONTENTS

CHAPTER I

CLUMSY SPIES

STANDING AT THE edge of the rotting wharf at Grand Marias, Jim Fallon filled his lungs with the sweet aroma of pine and spruce and cedar. East and west were long timbered shore lines stretching into the Northland, and at his feet were the chopping blue waters of Lake Winnipeg. Lashed to the edge of the wharf was the little wood-burning steamer that was to take him northward to Ross Island. His luggage was aboard and he was idling until sailing time.

The stifling cities of the States were behind Fallon. Now, as he leaned against the steady breeze that swept down upon him from the Northland, he felt new strength flowing into his muscular body. He drew his breath deeply and his blue eyes were eager.

On the last lap of the train trip to Grand Marias he had been aware of the guarded and seemingly hostile scrutiny of a good-looking young woman who sat across the aisle.

It left him slightly derisive. If she had any hope of his attempting to meet her gaze, she was wasting her time; for he had never had any enthusiasm over women who made a practice of hunting men. He did his own hunting, among women as well as in the wilderness fastnesses, and his fancy might lead him anywhere.

He had spent some years of his youth in the West—New Mexico, Arizona, Texas. He had punched cows in Wyoming and Montana; he had hunted gold in California and the Yukon,

1

and as yet no pretty face had stirred in him more than a passing interest.

He had not spoken to the woman, when a few minutes ago he had passed her at the farther end of the wharf. He had pretended not to see her, though he had been aware that her gaze had followed him.

He deliberately turned his back to her and devoted his attention to a scrutiny of the country. Timber; tundra with its rank growth of lichen and mosses; muskeg belts with their tall spears of marsh reeds; rolling hills and ridges; and an all-pervading atmosphere of somewhat mournful solemnity. It was enough to satisfy him. Space and silence, with adventure always lurking beyond the crest of the next ridge of land.

He heard a light step on the planking behind him, and was both amazed and amused when the woman stepped to within a few feet of him and addressed him.

"It *is* rather pretty, isn't it?"

Remembering her previous hostility, he glanced around curiously, certain that she had been speaking to some one near him. But the woman and himself were the only occupants of the wharf.

He looked at her, doffed his cap, and quietly agreed with her that the country was pretty.

The graceful lines of her figure were seductively emphasized by her short skirt and the light-weight checkered mackinaw. But she had passed her girlhood. Her complexion, the firmly rounded chin and throat, the mass of dusky golden hair, her general appearance, had misled him. Her eyes betrayed her.

Ingenuous as she sought to make them she did not quite succeed in creating in him the illusion that their owner was a frank, candid, guileless girl. Experience, sophistication, knowledge, lurked in their depths. And although Fallon was a gallant gentleman even with women he did not respect, there was a glint of cynicism in his eyes as he met her gaze.

"Is it always this pretty?" she asked. She was looking at his

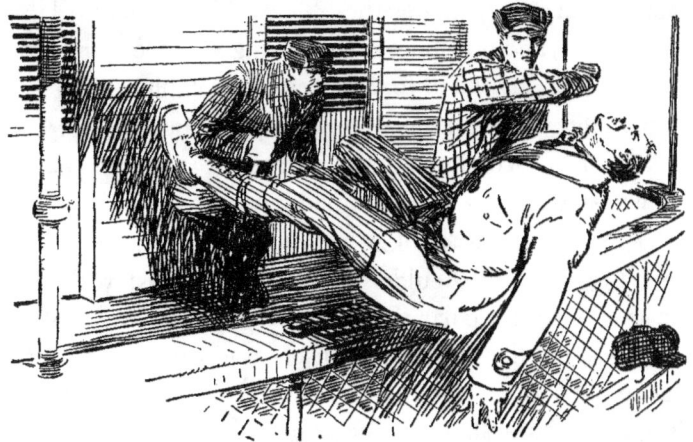

Fallon's attacker, unconscious, tumbled over the steamer rail.

broad shoulders as she spoke and he got the impression that she was estimating his physical strength. Why?

"Not always," he answered. "Not in the fall or the winter or the early spring. Just now it is in a gracious mood. It is like a woman's smile—not to be depended upon."

"My! I thought all sons of the wilderness were gallant! I find you are cynical… But—you know this country? You have been here before?"

"No."

HE LOOKED past her at the long, low rambling frame building which was used as a railway and steamboat station, storage house, freight depot. Boxes, crates, canoes, bales of goods, fishing nets and poles, were piled here and there in bundles, mounds and monuments. Above the building flew the red cross and caribou flag of a trading post.

From the door issued the indescribable odor of blending aromas from numerous unpacked food supplies. And in the doorway, which was wide and low, were two men who had ridden from Saint Boniface with the woman and Fallon. They had followed her into the train at Saint Boniface, and several times he had seen them together, talking. He had assumed they were friends, and now he was wondering why the woman did not join them instead of forcing herself upon him.

As Fallon glanced at them they were joined by the post trader, a squat, broad Scotchman in his shirt sleeves. He was hatless and was smoking a short-stemmed pipe.

The post trader was talking with one of the two men. The other, big, broad of shoulder and slender of waist, with arms and thighs so muscular that they bulged the sleeves of his mackinaw and the legs of his trousers, was leaning against the edge of the doorway, apart from his companion and the trader. He appeared to be staring at the planks of the wharf. But Fallon observed that he was in reality watching the girl and himself.

"You are the sort of man that likes adventure," she said.

Fallon looked again at the big man in the doorway and his lips curved slightly with contempt.

The woman did not see the smile. "Are you going far?"

He knew that if the two men and the woman were taking the steamer they would be aware when he left it. And so there was little to be gained by lying.

"Not far," he said. "I leave the steamer at Ross Island. After that I don't know."

"Have you friends at Ross Island?"

"Not a friend that I know of."

The woman smiled, but Fallon could see that she was vexed by his evasion of her questions, and perhaps by the fact that she was making no impression upon him. He might now have asked her some questions in return, but he resisted the impulse. If she and the men were what he thought, he could conduct his work more successfully by counterfeiting disinterest in their movements and by convincing them that his presence in the wilderness was purposeless.

The woman tapped the wharf with a small booted foot, and Fallon thought she was through with him. But no. She looked up at him again.

"They have some strange tales and legends in this country," she said. "I have heard several. Tales of great wolves—from the Barrens, I think; tribal superstitions that seem very ridiculous; stories of travelers that have disappeared; of fabulous mines that exist only until they are searched for. Coming up here on the train I was told a story about a gold mine so rich that it would make Midas envious. Do you think there is gold in this part of the country?"

"There are always rumors. I know of no great gold discoveries in this part of the country. Midas, eh? Well, Midas went out of business after the Yukon."

"You have been in the Yukon country?" She tried so carefully to conceal her eagerness.

He answered dryly: "A great many people were there."

"But you?"

He lied, shaking his head negatively.

She made a great effort to conceal her chagrin at his evasions.

"Perhaps I shall see you again, on the steamer," she said. "We are going to Ross Island, too."

She turned, left him.

FALLON walked to the farther end of the wharf. He was no longer amused. He saw the woman join the two men and walk slowly away from the building, the woman between the two men.

He wondered at the awkwardness of their methods. Obviously, they were novices. But there was earnestness in their manner, the tension of passion.

They went to the end of the wharf, away from Fallon. There they paused and the big man spoke to the woman. His voice was eager, vibrant.

"Well?" he said.

The woman's eyes were flashing with impotent rage. She clenched her hands and stood rigid. Her voice was harsh.

"It's no use."

"Not a word, eh?" said the big man. He grinned wryly and his lips curved back from his teeth. "Well, what did I tell you? It was a mistake to try to quiz him at all. We've put him next, now. Ever since we spotted him at Saint Boniface I've been trying to place him. I've got him now. It was the last grin he gave you. I'd seen it before. I saw it on his lips one night in a saloon in Dawson, when he made a gambler eat his gun. He's Jim Fallon!"

The other man started; his muscles seemed to leap and writhe. Then, his face paling, he stared disgustedly into the faces of his companions.

He cursed. "What a break! Another six months with no interference, and we'd have made the grade. If that man is all I've heard he is I'd rather have a fiend from hell on my trail!"

CHAPTER II

THE SHADOW OF A CLUB

THE LITTLE STEAMER was a flat-bottomed freighter, and there were no passengers aboard except the two men and the woman and Fallon when shortly before midnight she slipped away from the wharf and turned her prow northward to buck a stiff quartering head wind. Fallon alone kept the deck, to watch a white, brilliant moon rise and bathe the world with its magic, silver light.

The shore line slipped by. Beyond it stretched the wilderness, serene and calm, masking its dangers and hazards with the soft, hazy veil of distance; an empire of the wild.

This was the first time that Fallon had visited the Hudson Bay country, but from fellow travelers and adventurers on the rim of the Arctic Circle he had listened to tales that he had remembered; and in the office of a mining company in Montana he had listened to still another tale. A tale that was unforgettable, for the reason that weaving through it was a father's concern and affection for a son.

William J. Underhill, the mine owner, had a large tract of timber land along the Hayes River near Hudson Bay. Almost a year ago he had sent his twenty-five-year-old son, Linton Underhill, to look over the country.

"He wrote me from Selkirk that he had bought an outfit and engaged a guide," Underhill told Fallon. "The guide was a Chippewa Indian named 'Jackwoon.' Lin was starting right away. That was about a year ago.

"I didn't hear from him again. At first I thought he was in the wilderness and couldn't get to a post to get a letter out. After he had been gone about six months I made inquiries. The day my letter reached the post trader at Selkirk, the trader got word that the Indian guide had reported that Lin had disappeared.

"I've had a report from the police up there. The guide couldn't account for Lin's disappearance. He'd left a note for Jackwoon at a camp they had on the Shamattawa River near Merry Lake. I've got the note here."

He showed Fallon a piece of paper upon which were written, in pencil, the words:

JACK:
I am going north for a few days. Wait.

"There was no signature. But that's Lin's writing," resumed Underhill. "Naturally, there being only himself and the guide, he wouldn't bother to sign the note. Jackwoon told the police he had waited at the camp for two weeks, and when Lin didn't show up he worked back to the Hayes, trying to trail him. He couldn't find any trace of Lin.

"There's a man named Randall up there. He has built himself a big stone house in the wilderness north of the Hayes. He's a crank, I think; he must be, to build a house up there. He's wealthy, has big timber holdings north of the Hayes. The police reported that Randall had hired several outfits of Indian guides and runners to comb the country for Lin. The police and Randall and Lin's guide, Jackwoon, seem to have done all that can be done. But I am not satisfied. I feel that if I don't keep on trying to find Lin I won't be doing my duty as a father.

"And so I sent for you. If there's any man in the world who can find Lin, alive or dead, you are the man. Brave men, who do not know what defeat is, have recommended you. I wanted to have the best. Fallon, it isn't a question of money with you, I know, for you've all you need of that. I am told you take long chances because you like to match your wits and your courage and your muscle against conditions that seem to promise certain defeat.

"If I were thirty years younger I'd go up there myself. I know it's asking more than one man should ask of another, and I won't blame you a bit for refusing. But think it over, Fallon."

"I'm leaving to-night," was Fallon's reply. "I've wanted to take a look at that country, anyway, and this is as good a reason for going as any I can think of. But don't expect too much of me, Underhill. I'm vastly overrated. I've been lucky in pulling off three or four things that seemed to be difficult, to outsiders. They were actually rather simple. I'll go up there, but I won't promise how long I'll stay or what I shall do."

THAT conversation had taken place a little more than two weeks ago. In a pocket of Fallon's coat was a picture of Lin Underhill, and the note he had written to Jackwoon, the guide. The elder Underhill had wired Angus Mackenzie, the post trader at Grand Marias, to send Indian runners into the wilderness to search for Jackwoon and bring him back to Rossville to meet Fallon there.

Fallon refilled his pipe.

When he had been listening to Underhill in the latter's office in Montana he had been convinced that he was setting out on a hopeless quest. Linton Underhill had done a foolish thing in deserting his guide. The solution of the tragedy appeared to be simple. Lin, lost in the wilderness, had fallen victim to starvation, or wild animals, or one of the many savage nomadic tribes of Indians. Or he might have wandered into the muskeg to drown. There were many other ways in which a man might lose his life. A false step, a sudden illness, insanity.

But now Fallon was revising his convictions, for he knew that his meeting with the woman had not been casual or accidental. The big man, Fallon was certain, had urged the meeting. His lips curved cynically around the stem of his pipe. The big man's intelligence was not amazingly keen.

Did they have any inkling of his intentions? If so, was Lin

Underhill alive and held prisoner somewhere in the north country? Yet, what reason could any one have for holding him in captivity? The elder Underhill had offered no reward for Lin, nor had he received a demand for ransom. Now, having knocked the ashes from his pipe, he remembered that the woman had mentioned a gold mine. "A gold mine so rich that it would make Midas envious," she had said.

Was that the explanation—that they had discovered a mine and were afraid he had come north after it? Well, they would be relieved when they saw him leave the boat at Rossville and head eastward through the chain of lakes that led to the Hayes!

He got up and leaned against the rail while he watched the moonlight gleaming upon the water. As he put his pipe into a pocket he observed his shadow on the surface of the water and realized that it was past midnight. The moon was behind him, and the moonlight was so bright that he could even see the reflection of the boat's rail half a dozen feet out from the side.

And then, still gazing into the water, he saw another shadow join his on the surface—the shadow of a big man with broad shoulders.

He did not turn; he gave no sign that he knew the big man had come close to him. But when he saw an arm upraised in the shadow on the surface of the water he moved like a flash to the right and heard a club smash to splinters on the rail at the exact spot where his head would have been if he had not moved.

The weight of his body was on his toes as he ducked and slipped away. His lithe muscles were rippling with eagerness. He heard the shattered club splash into the water, and he saw the big man of the Grand Marias wharf plunge against the rail, momentarily off balance as his blow missed. The big man swung erect, amazed and uncertain. And in that instant Fallon flashed forward and swung his right arm in a full arc, pivoting in order to get into the blow the leverage of his body.

The fist landed with a splintering crash not unlike that which had been made by the club striking the rail, and the big man reeled backward with sagging knees.

Fallon was after him relentlessly. The thud and jar of the blows that landed on the big man's face could be heard above the throbbing of the engine. He was knocked hither and yon until he landed against the rail. He struck the rail with his hips. If he had been conscious he might now have grasped the rail and saved himself from the disaster that followed. But his body was limp and his brain deadened, and so he toppled backward and slid with a heavy splash into the water.

AS THE BIG MAN fell, another figure launched itself from the shadows of the deck house. It was not a club, but a knife, this time—for the blade rang on the deck as the man reeled along the rail from the effects of Fallon's smashing blow.

This man was smaller than the first, and only one blow was necessary. He fell, face down, on the deck near the rail. Fallon lifted him, swung him aloft and heaved him over the side, to join his companion.

It had been fast work, and Fallon stood at the rail, breathing deeply. He could see both men in the rippling, moonlit water. The shock had revived them and they were both swimming, a little astern. Fallon grimly watched them, but made no effort to help them. They needed something more cleansing than water, but for the present water would suffice.

And now came a voice from somewhere in the shadows of the deck house near the windward rail, crying hoarsely that there was a man overboard.

A bell rang, the noisy engine ceased throbbing. A man leaped from the wheel house, another came from the shadows of the deck house, the engineer emerged from his shallow hold and helped the others launch a small boat.

The victims of Fallon's smashing punches were far astern now, and were filling the night with their cries for help. Fallon watched the boat approach them; saw them pulled to safety.

Then he left the rail and went to his room, first picking up the knife and balancing it in his hand.

"Gold, eh?" he said, speculatively. "Well, yes; I've known of gold doing that to men."

CHAPTER III

BETRAYAL

FOR PERHAPS AN hour after Fallon stretched himself out in his bunk he was lying there trying to link his fragmentary thoughts into a direct chain of reasoning regarding the attack that had been made upon him.

The mere guess that he might be interested in a gold mine was too flimsy a structure upon which to base a murderous attack with a club and a knife.

He could not figure it out. The sensation of pleasant warmth that precedes sleep was stealing over him when he heard a voice coming into his berth from the half-open window.

The voice was low and guarded. It was pitched to harmonize with the whispering breeze and the soft moonlight.

"You saw it, eh?" said the voice.

"Saw it when it started," returned another voice. "I was stretched out on a bale of goods on the after deck house when I saw the big man—his name is Blandin—with a stick of timber, at least three inches thick. I was just opening my mouth to yell when Fallon ducked and smashed him. I never saw a man put so much steam into his punches.

"Soon as Fallon hit Blandin this other fellow, Kelso, rushed in. He dropped like a bag of meal. And then this Fallon picked him up like he was lifting a baby and heaved him over the side after Blandin. Seems Fallon was kind of stirred up over the way they'd come at him."

"Should think he would be," came the reply. "Fallon, you say his name is. Not Jim Fallon—the Klondike Fallon?"

"That's him. You've heard of him, eh?"

"Heard of him?" The voice was derisive. "Who hasn't heard of Klondike Fallon? He's one of the coolest and nerviest daredevils that ever drove a dog team near the Circle. So he handled Kelso like he was handling a baby, eh? He could do that. There's tales about his strength. Dead shot. A wizard with a knife. Can wear out half a dozen men on a trail. So that's Fallon, is it? Who has been telling you?"

"Angus Mackenzie. That Underhill man sent Fallon up here to find his boy."

"What about Blandin and Kelso and this woman; did old Angus tell you anything about them?"

"Only their names. The woman's named Devake. I heard Blandin call her Blanche."

"Sounds like a stage name. She—well, she ain't just the sort a man marries, is she?"

Both men laughed.

They were silent for a time and then one of them said:

"What do you suppose Fallon will do about them trying to murder him?"

"He won't do anything. As far as he's concerned, that affair is ended. Would you expect him to go to the police? Fallon ain't that kind. Whatever is done he will do himself."

The remainder of their conversation was not interesting to Fallon, though he went to sleep hearing their voices. After breakfast the next morning he went aft to smoke. The steamer was slow, but the shore astern had vanished. A brassy sun swam in a white sky and the wind had died. They went serenely past little timber-clad islands which were supremely calm and peaceful in their isolation; past wooded points that were boldly thrust out from the mainland. Bays, inlets, miles of marsh, rocky cliffs and timber-studded shore line came up, were passed and left behind.

There was a sameness in the landscape, and the atmosphere brought to one a sensation of vague and indefinable perturbation, as if the distances were immeasurable, and held elements that were mocking and waiting for an opportunity to pounce.

This spell that seized man was his dread and fear of the unknown. It pursues all men who thread the northern wilderness. It is the muted voice of the wild.

FOR PERHAPS an hour he sat there staring at the vessel's wake. Then he looked up to see the woman moving along the deck toward him. Her face was flushed, but her gaze was direct and defiant.

Fallon lifted his cap.

"Good morning, Miss Devake," he said.

"How did you learn my name?" she asked.

"I do not remember. It seems to me that you must have given it to me yesterday, on the wharf at Grand Marias."

"You are mistaken."

She had regained her poise. She was tranquil and serene, outwardly at least; and to Fallon, considering what had happened during the night, her manner proved that she was an adversary to be respected. The cool audacity lurking in the depths of her eyes as she faced him stirred him to something like wonder. Only a woman could have presented such self-control to an enemy. A man would have betrayed his feelings in some way.

"I must have learned it some way."

"We are even there, at least," she retorted coolly. "I know yours. You are Jim Fallon—Klondike Fallon."

"You got that from Mackenzie, eh?" He smiled at her. "You knew my name while you were trying to pump me."

"No. To tell the truth, I had an idea you were a greenhorn who had come up here to blunder into other people's business—until we pumped old Angus Mackenzie. Old man Underhill sent you up here to search for his missing son."

Fallon was silent. It would have been better if his mission could have been kept secret.

"You are a good man, Fallon," she resumed. "You are brave and resourceful and strong." A smile, reluctantly admiring and perhaps a bit wistful, tugged at her lips as she pronounced the final word, giving it emphasis by lingering upon it slightly.

"Then you heard of the midnight bathing incident," Fallon interjected.

"That was a mistake," she said. "I warned them not to try it. But they were determined. They insisted it was the only way to get rid of you."

"Attempted murder. And you made no effort to stop them. What's the meaning of it all? What do you care about young Underhill? If he's alive, why don't you let him communicate with his father? The man is frantic. If you've got him, why don't you set a price on him? Why all the mystery?"

She shook her head unsmilingly.

"You are smart, Fallon," she said. "But that is not the right way to get at it."

"PERHAPS not. But you certainly knew that if I were wiped out, Underhill would make at least one more search for the boy, and that he'd find some man who would be willing to do it."

"He'll not find another Jim Fallon."

"He doesn't need to. Jim Fallon is here."

"Yes," she said wryly, "we know it. But suppose Jim Fallon should spend two or three months up here minding his own business, and then would go back to Underhill and tell him that the search had been fruitless. And suppose that merely upon Jim Fallon's word that he would spend two or three perfectly idle months up here he would one day mysteriously receive fifty thousand dollars. Would that have any effect upon Jim Fallon?"

"It wouldn't thrill me at all, Blanche," he returned. He smiled at her. "It must be a big thing if you can offer fifty thousand."

"It's too big to lose, Fallon. And I warn you that we won't be interfered with. You don't know the country into which you are going. We do. They'll have a thousand chances to murder you, and they'll do it."

"I suppose I ought to thank you for warning me." He looked at her appraisingly, curiously. "Why did you warn me?" he added.

To his amazement he saw a flood of color steal up her neck and quickly diffuse itself over her cheeks and temples. She fought it, but in vain. Her eyes flashed and her lips curved with disdain and contempt. But the telltale color still flamed under the rouge.

"I've warned you because I hate you, Fallon!" she declared derisively.

She turned and walked rapidly away, leaving Fallon to stare into the empty distance while he meditated upon the inconsistencies of her sex.

He knew that she had developed some sort of a sentiment for him, despite the fact that he had not encouraged it; and he was now able to explain the hostility she had exhibited toward him in the beginning. She had then suspected him of prospective interference in her projects, but had instantly been attracted to him, and the hostility had been provoked by a fear that she would ultimately surrender to him, as women of her type have surrendered for hundreds of generations—as she had almost surrendered while standing there upon the deck.

Fallon's face grew long, for he had no desire to profit by a woman's weakness. But there it was—the revelation of their complicity. Either Lin Underhill had been murdered by these people and they were trying to keep the authorities from getting evidence that would convict them, or Lin was alive and they were holding him for some purpose which had not yet been revealed or suspected.

CHAPTER IV

THE CHIPPEWA GUIDE

THE LITTLE STEAMER nosed her prow, shortly after dawn of the second morning, into the log wharf at Rossville.

Upon all sides and reaching into the far distances, the scene upon which Fallon gazed would be a thousand times duplicated. Lakes and streams glittering like mirrors of steel, ranges of wooded hills, marshes and barrens, ranged away into immeasurable and incomprehensible space.

Blandin and Kelso and Blanche Devake were not to be seen, and Fallon suspected they were deliberately delaying their appearance until he should get out of the way, in the fear that he meant to report their attack upon him, but he had no such intention. He saw to the unloading of his dunnage, piled it against the wall of the trading post building, and sought the trader, Landieu, who had been standing in the doorway watching the steamer dock.

Landieu was tall, slender, courteous; and under his silken, graying mustache his white teeth gleamed as he smiled at Fallon.

Fallon returned the smile. He liked the trader, instantly. The man was a gentleman. He was quiet, slow of speech, and there was a manner about him that could not be acquired in one generation, but had to be inherited. Also, he was blessed with an intellect, for his fine, keen eyes had that knowing, confident gleam which is absent in the eyes of fools.

18

"You are Monsieur Fallon, of course. We have followed instructions. Jackwoon is here."

"Thank you, *monsieur*. Did your runners have trouble in locating him?"

"They do not say. But Jackwoon is here. Trouble, *m'sieur*, is not to be considered when a thing is to be done."

"Good. Monsieur Landieu has had experience."

"Monsieur Fallon has had experience, also. Great experience. Otherwise he would not be thinking of entering three hundred miles of the most terrible wilderness in the world."

"Jackwoon knows the country?"

Landieu shrugged his shoulders and smiled deprecatingly.

"Jackwoon is an Indian. What does he know? Who can tell? He was born on the Nelson. He is a Chippewa; he has a reputation. But what can be assured from that? He has been faithful, until—" He paused, smiled.

"Until Lin Underhill," said Fallon.

"Yes." Landieu watched the door, apparently fearful that his words would be overheard. His voice sank almost to a whisper.

"The young Underhill was with Jackwoon. *Pouf!* He vanishes! The note says he has gone north. Where? What is there in the north? Jackwoon knows the woods—every stream and river and lake, and every game trail. He can track the wolf and the lynx, and yet he cannot track a greenhorn, who would leave more signs than the moose. *M'sieur*, I feel there is something."

Fallon's brows drew together, but he said nothing. It had been at his suggestion that the elder Underhill had caused runners to be started into the wilderness to search for Jackwoon. He wanted Jackwoon to guide him down the Hayes, over the same trail that he had taken Lin Underhill. He wanted to watch Jackwoon; wanted to observe his movements, wanted to study him. He, too, had been suspicious of the Indian.

But Fallon was not thinking of taking any one into his confidence, not even Landieu.

HE MADE some inquiries about the country, about supplies. Then he walked to the door of the post building, leaned against one of the jambs and watched the gangplank of the steamer.

Blanche Devake and Kelso and Blandin were stepping down to the wharf. The woman came first, and for an instant her gaze met Fallon's. She gave no indication that she had seen him.

Blandin descended. His lips were swollen grotesquely, and his eyes were sullen as he caught sight of Fallon, though Fallon stared past him. Kelso's eyes were purple and puffed, and almost closed. He did not look at Fallon, but bent his head and pretended to be interested in the luggage that was piled on the wharf near him.

The three were on the wharf only a few minutes. They presently moved off and Fallon saw them walking toward a hut near which half a dozen dogs were snarling and fighting.

"*Sacré nom!*" ejaculated Landieu, at Fallon's shoulder. "*M'sieur* is not fastidious about his fellow-travelers!"

"You know them, eh?" said Fallon.

"They have been here before, *m'sieur*. Once last year, and once before, this year. They go east, to the Randall château."

Fallon's eyelashes flickered and the keen-eyed post trader smiled.

"*M'sieur* has heard of the stone château?"

"It has been mentioned in my presence."

"*M'sieur* is discreet," said Landieu. "It is well. They go down the Hayes, also, *m'sieur*."

"Friends of Randall?"

"Ah! I do not know. One supposes they are friends or they would not visit so often. But does it not make one wonder at Monsieur Randall, that he should have such friends?"

"Randall has a good reputation?"

"The best. That is what makes it strange."

Landieu did not add to this, so Fallon inquired about Jackwoon.

The Indian, sitting on the edge of the low wharf, was pointed out to him. Jackwoon appeared to be indifferent to his surroundings. His legs were dangling over the edge of the wharf, and he was hunched up, smoking a short-stemmed pipe.

Landieu hailed him, telling him to come and meet the man who had engaged his services, and Jackwoon, civil and quiet, and deliberate of movement, approached and was introduced to Fallon.

Jackwoon was short and heavy. He was not fat, but muscular. There was strength in his broad shoulders and in his thick arms and wrists. His face was broad, his forehead low, and his straight black hair was smoothed and greased so that it emphasized the flatness of his head. His nose was big. His eyes, black, lambent, sly, met Fallon's briefly. His lips smiled shallowly.

" **WHERE** M'sieur Fallon go?" he asked, employing the macaronic jargon in which alone it is possible for the Indian and white man to converse.

"Down the Hayes."

"How far go?"

The black eyes darted a glance into Fallon's—a probing, searching glance which would perhaps enable him to discover something about the character of the big white man who had sought him out.

What Jackwoon saw was a pair of steady blue eyes which were entirely lacking in warmth. Whatever was in them was not for Jackwoon to see; a baffling vacuity which could not be penetrated or analyzed. There was no antagonism, no friendliness, no emotion whatever in them.

Jackwoon's gaze wavered, drooped.

"To where you lost Underhill," said Fallon. "How far is that?"

"Ten sleep, mebbe." He smiled apologetically. "Jackwoon good guide. Underhill man know too much—no listen."

"All right," said Fallon. "Where is your canoe?"

Jackwoon pointed to a sloping, stony beach where a light

canoe was drawn up, and then stood listening while Fallon bought a second canoe from Landieu.

"All right, Jackwoon; we'll split the load," said Fallon. He strode to where his dunnage was piled, separated it and pointed to the portion the guide was to take.

"You go now?" questioned the latter. "You got grub?"

"Right away."

Landieu slid out a canoe equipped with paddle and pole, and then went inside with Fallon, where the food supply was selected and packed.

An hour later Jackwoon, somewhat reluctantly, it seemed, pushed off in his canoe and deftly swept it outward from the shore, where he permitted the craft to float idly in the current while he watched Fallon. His face was inscrutable, but his eyes quickened when he observed that the white man's movements were as certain and definite as his own.

A wave of the hand by Fallon, a low *"Le Bon Dieu* be with you," from Landieu standing on the wharf, and they were off, with Jackwoon heading his craft straight down the channel toward the vast wilderness beyond.

As the paddles flashed in the bright sunlight, smoothly slipping in and out of the mirror-like surface of the water, Landieu turned and gazed back toward the land.

In front of the hut to which they had gone directly after leaving the steamer, stood Blandin, Kelso and Blanche Devake.

They were watching Jackwoon and Fallon, who were already far down the channel.

CHAPTER V

A TRAP FOR A LIAR

JACKWOON PADDLED STEADILY, driving his canoe ahead with slow, graceful sweeping strokes that sent the light craft skittering over the water like a dry leaf in a breeze. The Indian did not look back.

A hundred yards behind came Fallon's canoe, handled as capably as the Indian's. There was seemingly no effort in Fallon's movements—in his sliding, dipping, deftly-turned strokes that created only a gently swirling eddy on the surface of the water.

Jackwoon's failure to glance back was significant. It told Fallon that already the Indian had appraised him and had decided he was experienced. If he had betrayed awkwardness in getting his canoe off, or if his handling of the paddle had revealed lack of skill, Jackwoon would have shown some interest in him.

Rossville was the last settlement they would encounter until they reached Hudson Bay—if they went that far. On some far waterway there might be a trading post, but if there was, Fallon had no knowledge of it. And when they had traveled three or four miles down the channel a jutting shoulder of the mainland shut Rossville from their view and they were in the wilderness.

They went on, skimming the mirror-like surface of the water, past innumerable small timbered islands. At noon they were on the slender stream that connects the channel with Pipestone Lake, and at dusk the keels of their canoes grated slightly on

the pebbly gravel and sand of a small midstream island which
was featured by ice-polished bowlders and tufts of black willow.

It was Fallon who selected the island as a camping place for
the night. Jackwoon had mutely pointed to a sloping beach on
the mainland southward, but Fallon had shaken his head in
dissent.

The canoes were beached and the cargo unpacked. Jackwoon
soon had a fire going, and while he was engaged in cooking
supper Fallon inspected the island, which was an oblong piece
of land about a hundred yards wide at its broadest part and
probably two hundred yards long.

There was little current in the river; the water was smooth
and glassy, and the silence sepulchral. After supper Fallon
stretched himself on a rock near the fire and smoked. Jackwoon,
having washed the cooking utensils and restored them to their
bag, was squatted near the fire. He also was smoking, and his
wide, flat face was expressionless.

All day Fallon had studied the Indian; and now, across the
fire, he was again attempting to solve the enigma of the man's
character.

He knew, however, that he had made little progress. Innocent
or guilty, noble or ignoble, the Indian masks his feelings with
a stoic indifference which is not to be penetrated. Whatever
Jackwoon knew about the disappearance of Lin Underhill he
would keep to himself. He would evade straight or direct questions and he would not be trapped by oblique ones.

And yet one thing had Fallon observed, and he got a mali-
cious satisfaction out of the knowledge: Jackwoon was uncomfortable in his presence. His attempts to conceal the fact only
resulted in making his condition more apparent to the observing eyes that watched him.

So far, Fallon had not spoken a dozen words to Jackwoon,
and he did not speak now as he smoked and studied the Indian's face, which was illumined by the ruddy glow of the fire.
But Jackwoon was aware that he was being watched, and he
was uneasy.

AN HOUR passed. Fallon had not moved except to refill his pipe. Jackwoon still squatted near the fire, which he replenished from time to time.

The darkness deepened; the white light in the north sank close to the horizon. Reddish-tinted stars came out; the black forests on all sides grew to a denser black and seemed to creep nearer. A lynx screamed like a woman being subjected to excruciating torture. A wolf howled.

Jackwoon had been uncomfortable all day, with the knowledge that the keen-eyed white man had been watching him. Most white men who had come under Jackwoon's observation talked more or less. This man—this Fallon—did not talk except when he gave orders. He was lying on the rock now, staring. Jackwoon did not look at him, but he could feel Fallon's gaze; and he knew that if he looked up now Fallon's cold, steady gaze would be fixed upon him.

A strange man, Fallon. The primitive mind of the Indian was awed by the power and force he felt in this white man. He grew more uneasy.

And then, like a whisper, low and gentle, it came—Fallon's voice:

"Was Underhill a good man?"

"Um. Him good man. But him know too much. Go 'lone. Not know country."

"You were in camp?"

"Yes. One sleep."

"Underhill leave at night?"

"In morning. We want meat. I go hunt. Come back noon—him gone."

"Which way?"

"Him go north."

"Where was the camp?"

"On Shamattawa. Merry Lake."

"Where had you been?"

"Come back from south."

"Where were you going?"

"To Hayes River. Fox River, mebbe. Underhill say look for more timber."

"Meet anybody? White man—Indian?"

"Indian—one time, two time. Know 'em."

"No white men?"

Jackwoon's answers had up to this time been given instantly. Now he hesitated. The hesitation was only momentary, but it was enough to convince Fallon that the Indian was considering his answer.

"No white men. Indian; Cree."

"Underhill good hunter?"

"Him no hunt."

"Carry rifle?"

"In canoe. Carry on portage."

"How do you know he went north?"

"Find tracks."

"How far from Shamattawa to Hayes?"

"Seventy, eighty mile."

"Underhill take grub?"

Jackwoon shook his head negatively.

"Take rifle?"

"Him take rifle. Go hunt, mebbe. Get lost. Mebbe no grub for week or two. Him no good shoot."

"You saw him shoot?"

"Him shoot at deer. So times." Jackwoon held up his hand and separated the fingers until he had counted four. "No hittum," he added.

"He load rifle again after he missed the deer?"

"Him rifle always loaded."

"How far did you track him?"

"Lose him ten, fi'teen mile. Big rain. Go north, anyway. No

find. Me go Fox River, to Randall. Big hunt—Randall, Indian. No find. Go back to canoe—to Landieu. Give Landieu Underhill man stuff. Talk police. Underhill man lost. No find."

"Too bad," said Fallon. He was silent for a time. The fire grew low, its light dimmed. Then suddenly, from the darkness of the rock Fallon fired another question—sharp, stern:

"What did Blandin say?"

In the dying firelight Fallon saw the stoic calm of Jackwoon's face disturbed by a quick tightening of the lips. He was startled. He spoke hesitatingly.

"Blandin say Underhill man—" He paused, his face grew blank. He shook his head with a violent negative. "Jackwoon not know Blandin man. Mebbe see; not know."

"What did Blandin say?"

"Say Underhill man lost, mebbe."

"Who did he say that to?"

"Randall, mebbe. Hear him say. Forget."

"At Randall's place?"

Jackwoon shook his head. "No can think."

"Blandin was up here last year. You see him?"

"See um, mebbe. No talk um."

"Blandin had a guide?"

"Ugh. Kumwa—him Cree. More." Jackwoon held up four fingers.

Fallon did not ask any more questions. He now knew that the Indian had been implicated in the disappearance of Lin Underhill, but he had been instructed, perhaps bribed, to pretend ignorance.

There had been the stupefied expression of the Indian's face when he realized that he had committed himself about Blandin. Moreover, there was something that Fallon had not mentioned to Jackwoon. Fallon had examined the effects belonging to Lin Underhill, and had found two hundred rifle cartridges. The boxes containing them were unbroken. And Landieu's itemized list of the supplies bought by Lin revealed that only two hundred cartridges had been purchased.

Lin's gun was of heavier caliber than Jackwoon's, and so obviously Lin had not borrowed cartridges from the Indian. Jackwoon had lied about Lin having used the rifle and about his having taken it with him when he had disappeared.

However, Fallon did not divulge his knowledge to the Indian. He had discovered enough to convince him that there was a secret understanding between Blandin and Jackwoon, and that he might expect further attacks by Blandin, and disloyalty from the Indian.

CHAPTER VI

WHITE WATER

DURING THE NEXT few days Fallon and Jackwoon made several short portages and one long one; and on these Jackwoon tested the mettle of the white man. Without looking back, he moved with his utmost speed, an effort that taxed his toughened muscles and stamina, as he sought to outdistance Fallon.

He never succeeded. If the portage was a mile or ten miles, he always found Fallon at his heels when he halted or when the portage ended. Amazed and sullen, he was compelled to admit that Fallon's strength and stamina were greater than his own.

Because of his pride, Jackwoon would be extravagantly deliberate in lowering his pack and setting his canoe down, knowing that an exhibition of haste would betray his weariness to the white man. But after the load was off his shoulders he would not be able instantly to straighten his cramped legs. Fallon could not fail to realize his condition.

He watched keenly for like signs of weakness or weariness in Fallon's movements, but he observed none. Fallon appeared to be tireless. He would drop his pack carelessly, swing his canoe off his shoulders with marvelous ease and dexterity, flex his great muscles like an athlete going through setting-up exercises, and expand his great chest with obvious delight. At such times his blue eyes would dance with exultation.

A great man, conceded Jackwoon. A white god. Never had he seen another like him. There was in Jackwoon a reluctant admiration, restrained and tempered by the hatred that is engendered by the consciousness of inferiority.

Fallon had ceased talking. But he had not ceased watching Jackwoon, gazing steadily at him out of an enigmatic silence.

Day by day Jackwoon grew more uneasy. And day by day his hatred of Fallon grew. He began to wonder about ways and means of getting rid of Fallon. There were many ways, of course. The only thing that deterred him was the conviction that he would not succeed, that Fallon was somehow invulnerable.

They were on the Hayes River, paddling down a gorge between two small lakes, when the dark thought came to Jackwoon. At first it startled him, for it was nothing short of an inspiration. Then as he sent the canoe swiftly down the stream he dwelt upon the idea, considering it well. In the end he decided to act upon it.

The stream was here smooth and wide and deep. The current was lazy, but he, who had paddled down it many times, knew of its powerful lower current, knew that the water felt the pull of the tearing, rushing rapids not more than two or three miles distant.

A few—a very few—times had the rapids been shot with a canoe. Jackwoon had achieved the feat once, but he knew he would never try it again. There was a channel, to be sure, and he had found it. But the finding had been merely accidental; his ultimate escape from the huge, hidden rocks having resulted from the fact that in his fright he had done nothing more than to permit the canoe to race with the current. He had seen the rocks, had felt them merely touch the sides and bottom of his craft, as he had flashed past them on the crests of the boiling waves that swirled and eddied like a mad thing in the agonies of death.

And now Jackwoon's eyes glittered. Now he would see if the white man were invulnerable—if his gods could keep this death from him.

He had not told Fallon about the rapids. And now, already

feeling the surface pull of the current, he made not a motion that might be construed as apprehension or preparation. He did not shift his position or turn his head.

HALF a mile from the rapids the current seized them and bore them along swiftly, faster than either man could paddle. A paddle could not increase the speed of their canoes, and was of use only as a rudder. The stream made a sharp bend to the right, and the big granite walls around which the water surged concealed the rapids from view until one was almost upon them.

Jackwoon knew exactly what Fallon's intelligence would impel him to do. He could do nothing less—and nothing more. And as Jackwoon's craft sped along the curving walls he observed out of the corners of his eyes that the white man was striving to drive closer; the swiftness of the current had warned him.

He thought just what Jackwoon wanted him to think—that Jackwoon's purpose was to run the rapids. And now, cunningly, the Indian used his paddle, retarding slightly the speed of his craft. He knew that the white man would believe his guide's purpose was to permit him to draw closer, to keep his canoe close in the wake of the guide's.

When the white water came into sight, Jackwoon made his first sign, a signal to apprise the white man of danger. He moved his left hand slightly outward, as though pushing something invisible, warning Fallon to keep out from the granite walls. If Fallon did that—if he permitted his canoe to be seized by the current in the center of the river—he would not be able to drive his canoe out of it before he reached the white water. And if the white water caught him, his gods would have to take the paddle into their hands. Fallon obeyed his signal.

It was done quickly. At the edge of the white water Jackwoon swiftly swung the prow of his canoe around and drove it shoreward, into a sheltered lagoon out of the current, where the water calmly swirled against a low, sloping shore line.

He saw Fallon's canoe shoot by. He caught a glimpse of the

white man's face; met the glint of contempt in his eyes; noted with silent fury a grim smile curving his lips. And then Fallon was in the white water, and the spume was covering him like a white, fleecy veil.

Jackwoon sat long in his canoe at the edge of the sloping beach. He was smiling vindictively. No more uneasiness; no more of feeling his back muscles cringe and writhe with the white man's gaze upon him; no more sitting across from Fallon at the camp fire, not daring to lift his gaze from the embers.

He'd go back now, to Rossville, to Landieu, and report Fallon's death. An accident, of course. Fallon had been determined to shoot the rapids, even after he had been told of the danger.

Jackwoon was very deliberate now. There was time. He landed, dragged his canoe to the sloping beach, got his pack ready, swung it from his shoulders, balanced the canoe and set off over the portage that he always used in going around the rapids.

It was not a very difficult portage, but it was rather long, for it led down a slope away from the river for quite a distance, then circled back to the smooth water a mile from the rapids.

It was Jackwoon's curiosity that was sending him to the still water, where he might find Fallon's body and the wreck of his canoe. Jackwoon would spend the night there, perhaps, watching the dark waters by the light of his fire, gloating over the death of the white man whose strength and spirit had *seemed* unconquerable. This white man who was so wise and yet had been led to his death by the waving of a hand.

Exultant, grinning his triumph, and moving with care and deliberation lest he make a false step and bring retribution upon himself for his deed, he came down the long, circling slope toward the level land at the edge of the smooth water. There was some scraggly spruce here, and some poplar and black willow. This growth obstructed his view of the river edge for some time. But when he got through it and got a clear view of the bank, his knees sagged with sudden weakness and he almost fell.

For there, sitting on the bank, calmly smoking his pipe, was Fallon!

JACKWOON'S muscles grew rigid again. His brain flamed with a great wrath. He made no sound, however, but merely stood there staring.

Apparently Fallon was not aware of Jackwoon's presence. His back was toward the Indian. He was sitting on a pebbly slope with his knees drawn up. His arms were folded over his chest, and he seemed to be interestedly watching the smoothly swirling water. His canoe had been pulled up on the bank, away from the water.

Jackwoon's rage and disappointment stirred him to a murderous impulse. He was trembling with eagerness now, but he managed to swing canoe and pack from his shoulders. The rifle he always carried was under the pack straps. He slipped it out, sat down on the pack, raised the rifle to his shoulder and took steady aim at Fallon's broad back. He pressed the trigger—and heard the firing pin click futilely, metallically.

He sat, stupefied, and saw Fallon turn his head and look at him with level gaze.

"No use, Jack," Fallon said. "I took them out several days ago. And there are no more in your pack. I took them, too. They are a good many miles back."

Jackwoon's muscles turned to water as he sat on the pack with his mouth open. The rifle dropped from his nerveless hands. Awe, and a nameless terror, had seized him. He would die here. Presently Fallon would draw out his own rifle and begin to shoot. He'd do it calmly, as he did everything.

But for a few minutes nothing happened. Then Fallon turned over on his stomach, and Jackwoon observed that while Fallon had been sitting there he had had a rifle between his knees. The weapon was in his hands now and was carelessly aimed at the

Indian. Fallon now spoke, and his voice had a ring of cold contempt in it.

"You have forgotten your gods, eh, Jack?"

Jackwoon did not answer. He could think of nothing to say. He was not afraid now. He had a fatalistic conviction that he was to die in this place, where he had twice attempted the white man's life. Two failures were enough. And so he sat, his eyes sullen, his lips in a heavy pout, returning Fallon's gaze. His gods had indeed deserted him.

"Shoot," Jackwoon said.

"Presently."

For a long time Fallon was silent. He watched Jackwoon's face over the barrel of the rifle. He moved the muzzle slowly. He seemed to be undecided. Twice the muzzle covered the Indian's heart; once it was directed at his stomach; half a dozen times it was pointed directly at his forehead, for staring at the muzzle he could look along the barrel.

The white man's steady eyes were on the sights; and with death imminent, Jackwoon wondered and marveled at Fallon's cold nerve.

"How old are you, Jack?" he said.

"Thirty-four summers,"

"Married?"

"Me got squaw."

"Papoose?"

"No."

"Well, if you die now it won't make any difference. Maybe squaw like you now. Maybe when you die she'll get another brave. There's always another brave, Jack."

Jackwoon's lips formed a word, but gave forth no sound. White Bear! Fallon was right; many times had Jackwoon's heart been torn by jealousy of White Bear. For he had observed how White Bear's eyes quickened when they rested upon his woman; when his death was established as a certainty White Bear would make the advances he had long meditated.

FALLON had observed Jackwoon's hesitation; he saw the dark blood steal into Jackwoon's face, and down again, to coagulate and burn at heart. Cunningly, with a deep knowledge of the elementary passions of Jackwoon, learned by his constant scrutiny and study of the Indian during the days and nights of their journey, Fallon had struck the chord that had set his heart to tingling with a desire to live.

But not at once did Jackwoon speak. Nor did Fallon interfere with his mental processes. The silence between them grew long.

"White man no shoot. Jackwoon sorry."

The words came slowly, reluctantly. But the sullen eyes were gleaming hopefully.

"You want to live, eh?"

A nod.

"All right. You live. How long, depends upon how you answer some questions. Is Lin Underhill alive?"

Jackwoon nodded.

"Where is he?"

"Not know."

"Who took him away?"

"Blandin. Kelso. Indian." Jackwoon held up four fingers.

"Blandin, Kelso and four Indians?"

A nod.

"They took him from your Shamattawa camp?"

"Yes."

"Was Underhill hurt?"

"No."

"Where did they take him?"

"Not know. Up north."

"What did Blandin say?" Fallon repeated the question he had asked Jackwoon several days ago.

"Blandin say they no hurt Underhill. Blandin say give Jackwoon new rifle, canoe, plenty gold soon if keep mouth shut. Get rifle, canoe. No get gold."

"That's why you tried to kill me. The gold hasn't been paid, and you thought it wouldn't be paid if I interfered…. Where does Randall live?"

"Little Fox—Big Fox."

"How far?"

"One sleep down river. Three sleep north."

Fallon was silent. He was silent so long that Jackwoon grew cold with a dread that sat so heavily upon him that it bowed his shoulders. Then, finally, Fallon got up. Slowly he stood erect and stretched his great arms.

"All right, Jack," he said, "let's go."

He walked to his canoe, slipped the rifle into the pack straps, pushed the canoe into the water and shoved out into the current. He paddled lazily, holding the canoe against the current until Jackwoon launched his own craft and swung down the river ahead of him.

Lin Underhill had not been killed by his abductors. The fact that Blanche Devake had offered fifty thousand dollars proved conclusively to Fallon that the purpose was to obtain from Underhill a large amount of money, by ransom or by taking possession of the gold that Lin Underhill had acquired since he had come into the country.

Fallon had some reason to think the latter, for no ransom demand had reached the elder Underhill, and Fallon had not forgotten that the Devake woman had mentioned a mine "that would make Midas envious."

Fallon was pleased. This expedition was not to be a search for a dead man; it was to be a battle for a life and a fortune—for two lives, his own and Lin Underhill's. Arrayed against him were two unscrupulous white men and all the lawless red men that could be bought or bribed. It might be that even the somewhat mythical Randall would develop into an enemy.

Fallon was headed into a mysterious country. A few hundred feet in front of him was a faithless guide, behind him were two men who had already revealed their murderous purpose, and upon all sides as he pushed further into the wilderness would be the hazards of the silent coverts from which might be sped the winged arrow of the white men's forest confederates.

CHAPTER VII

AMBUSH

SINCE FALLON HAD discovered that Lin Underhill was alive and had been taken north, he told Jackwoon to head straight down the Hayes until he reached a point directly north of where Lin had been captured.

Late in the afternoon they entered a section of river where there were several islands. The mainland was featured by low, rolling, timber-clad hills which swept down to the water and were fringed by a rank growth of marsh weeds, huge granite rocks and willows.

The islands were comparatively bare except for evergreen clumps here and there. Fallon selected one of them for a camp, drove his canoe upon a sloping beach and called to Jackwoon.

Dusk had come by the time Jackwoon had prepared supper. They ate in silence, and then Fallon got up, stepped to the river with the frying pan in hand, filled the pan with water, and carefully drowned the fire. Jackwoon said nothing, but watched interestedly.

Fallon sat on a rock and smoked. It was dark now, and Fallon went behind a huge bowlder to light his pipe; he was careful to cup the blaze of the match with his hand. Over the bowl of the pipe he observed Jackwoon watching him. A fleeting glance, then Jackwoon looked down again.

Later, a match blazed in Jackwoon's hand and was applied to his pipe. The match flared brightly, revealing the Indian's flat features and his black, gleaming eyes. The eyes were defiant.

Fallon laughed—and threw himself backward behind the bowlder where he had lighted his pipe, at just the instant that a rifle bullet, fired from the south bank of the river, struck the rock, glanced off and went whining into the trees on the north shore.

At the noon halt Fallon had buckled on a cartridge belt, a holster and a huge Colt revolver which he took from his pack. Jackwoon had watched this ominous proceeding, and he should have taken heed of the threat it portended.

He had no time to regret his action in lighting the match so that its blaze would reveal Fallon to his friends on the south shore. For as Fallon threw himself backward, the big gun at his hip crashed heavily.

Jackwoon, throwing himself sidewise, received the bullet in his right arm, near the shoulder. He pitched forward to the rocks, screaming curses, as Fallon's gun roared again, and a naked Indian, looming out of the darkness behind Jackwoon, plunged forward and landed heavily beside him.

The rifle on the south shore was silent now, but as Fallon rose to his feet he heard a crunching of the pebbles on the beach behind him; saw a dark figure silhouetted against the star haze.

He bent his body from the hips and heard a caribou spear hiss over him and shiver itself against the huge bowlder behind him. His Colt roared again and the dark figure vanished. A knife clattered on the rocks near the shore; there was a splash in the water that sent a fine spray upward. The spray dissolved, the darkness held no more figures; silence again reigned.

FOR A TIME Fallon did not move. Jackwoon, the treacherous, did not again raise his voice. Fallon crept forward on his hands and knees and found the knife that had been dropped by the Indian who had fallen into the water, ran an investigating hand over the weapon, and slipped it into his belt. From its feel he identified it as a long, ivory-handled *kiliutok* knife. It was wet, and he knew the Indian owner had swum to the island with his confederate who had died behind Jackwoon.

He fired at the Indian's dark figure.

There had been three of the Indians. Away back at the edge of the smooth water near the rapids, Fallon had seen them, portaging their canoes through the timber. That was why, at the smooth water, he had forgiven Jackwoon so quickly.

Twice during the day he had seen them again, as they lurked behind on the river; and several times in the dark green foliage of the trees far back from the river's edge, he had caught the reflection of the sun gleaming on their paddles. The mirror-like flashes were unmistakable, and he had been able to determine with some accuracy how far they were behind him.

Just at dusk, far up the river, he had seen some tall rushes waving. Twice they had been agitated, and he knew the three Indians had two canoes.

When he had poured water on the fire he had observed Jackwoon's lips droop disappointedly; and when he had mutely communicated to Jackwoon his knowledge of the presence of the Indians on the south shore—by lighting his pipe in the shelter of the huge bowlder—Jackwoon had defiantly lighted his own in the open, thus exposing Fallon to the fire of the waiting enemy.

In the faint star haze Fallon could see Jackwoon and the first Indian he had killed. The savage, naked except for a breechcloth, was lying face down on a slab of rock, the starlight gleaming on his greased body. Jackwoon was sitting, bent forward, his left hand gripping his right arm. He tried to stifle a groan, but did not succeed.

"Hurts, eh?" said Fallon unconcernedly. "Well, you were lucky, Jack. My elbow struck a rock when I pulled on you, or you'd have been with your friend there."

He now told Jackwoon to light another match and to motion, while the match blazed, to the remaining Indian on the south shore. Then Jackwoon was to sit down again.

Jackwoon obeyed. Apparently there was no instinct or impulse of loyalty in him. He sat down again after lighting the match, and waited.

He had not long to wait. Listening, both men could hear the water rippling as the prow of a canoe cleaved it. They could hear the keel of the light craft grate slightly upon the sloping shore.

Jackwoon did not look, but he heard a light step behind him, and he shivered and cringed when Fallon's heavy revolver belched a crimson lance that passed above him. He heard the Indian groan as he fell, and after that there came no sounds except the gentle lapping of the water against the shore and the voices of the denizens of the timber.

CHAPTER VIII

THE SECRET CHANNEL

THE KILLING OF the third Indian was necessary and Fallon felt no remorse for the deed. He had meant to kill Jackwoon, too; he had told the Indian the truth about his elbow striking a rock at the instant he had pressed the trigger. For Jackwoon had been disloyal and treacherous.

Twice had Fallon obeyed an impulse of mercy when for his own safety he should have killed a would-be murderer: once when Blandin and Kelso had attacked him on the steamer and again when Jackwoon had tried to shoot him when his back was turned.

In Fallon was now stirring the primitive passion of self-preservation; and, augmented by this latest attack upon him by his enemies, Blandin and Kelso, there grew the cold determination to fight these men by the methods they themselves had introduced; a cold calm that masked turbulent passions.

He did not sleep. He sat there, facing Jackwoon through the short night. When the first gray streaks lighted the eastern sky he got up, and scouted around the edge of the island.

He unloaded Jackwoon's canoe, laid the pack on the ground, opened it and removed everything that belonged to the Indian. To these he added grub enough to last for two or three days.

Then he added the remainder of the Indian's pack to his own effects, distributing the load in the canoe so that it would ride evenly when his own weight was in it; stepped on the shore again and looked at his sullen-eyed guide.

"You're through, Jack," he said. "No good. You stay here. In one, two days, maybe, Blandin and Kelso will come. The grub I'm leaving will last you until then."

Jackwoon did not answer. He sat, staring at the ground.

Fallon took up a bowlder that must have weighed at least a hundred pounds, carried it to where the Indian's canoe was drawn up on the shore, laid the bowlder down, and shoved the canoe into the water. Picking up the bowlder again, he dropped it into the center of the craft, smashing its keel and knocking a great hole in its side. He treated the other likewise.

He pushed his own canoe into the water, and paddled downstream, to disappear from Jackwoon's view. Presently he reappeared, heading across the river to the south shore.

In some rushes he found the second canoe belonging to the Indians. After wrecking it he shot his own craft out into the current and vanished among the islands downstream.

He apprehended no further immediate danger from Blandin's hirelings. He had no doubt that Blandin and Kelso were several days behind him, and that they would travel slower than he, with three in the party—if they brought Blanche Devake with them.

ALTHOUGH his canoe was now laden with almost all the luggage it still did not carry more than an ordinary load, and skimmed the water lightly under the impetus of his powerful strokes.

Jackwoon, loyal or neutral, would have been a help to him but disloyal he was a burden and a menace. Without a guide his difficulties would be multiplied; he was a stranger to the country. But he was wise with years spent in wilderness sections as vast and as desolate as this.

He shot swiftly through a gorge between towering rock walls into a broad stretch of smooth water several hundred yards wide and seemingly two or three miles long.

The sun was high now, and it shone straight down the river eastward into Fallon's eyes. He drove the canoe toward the north shore, into the shadows. The water was deep and his canoe sped swiftly along the glassy surface.

He blinked his eyes rapidly and held his paddle poised, permitting the canoe to glide along unguided while he stared, amazed and incredulous, almost convinced that what he saw was a thought-picture, a day-dream.

Not more than two hundred yards ahead of him, straight down the stream and shooting rapidly shoreward, was a canoe with a woman in it. She had seen him apparently for she was bending forward, plying the paddle furiously, evidently seeking cover before he should see her. And while he watched, her canoe slipped past a rocky point and vanished.

His glance at the woman had been brief, and she was too far away for him to be able to distinguish her features, but she wore a checkered mackinaw, a white stocking cap, and when for an instant the sunlight had shone on her hair he had caught a glint of gold in it.

The woman was Blanche Devake, of course, he decided. But how could she have reached this place so soon? Naturally, if the Devake woman was here, Blandin and Kelso were also in the vicinity. Was there another waterway through the wilderness, or were they familiar with some trail which had brought them across country?

FALLON'S hesitation lasted only a few minutes. He was aware of the danger of ambush. However, they would not need to prepare such a trap, for if they had been informed that he was coming straight down the river they had only to conceal themselves and shoot him as he passed. Besides, the woman's fright at sight of him had seemed to be real. She had been so startled that she had rocked the canoe, and with her first stroke had almost dropped the paddle, and she had subsequently displayed every evidence of terror. The canoe had swayed from side to side under the impetus of her splashing and hurried strokes.

Fallon had decided. He drove his canoe to the point of rocks, deftly turned it shoreward and permitted it to glide into a little bay formed by the rocky point and the mainland. His heavy revolver was in his right hand.

He was a fair target for an enemy on shore, and still nothing happened. The smooth water of the little bay was still slightly ruffled by the passing of the woman's canoe, but the craft and its occupant were not in sight.

The mainland was fringed by a dense growth of various varieties of cedar, pine, spruce, fir and willows so wild and thick that a man would have trouble trying to penetrate it. Fallon's gaze searched the marsh reeds along the shore, the rocks of the point around which he had come. He could see no place where a canoe had landed.

He paddled slowly toward the deeper recesses of the bay. In the center of the bay there was deep water, and it continued deep clear to the end of the bay. This unusual condition was explained when he observed that the bottom was composed of huge blocks of rock which had probably been tossed there centuries ago during some gigantic upheaval of the earth. There had been no delta-building stream here.

He had allowed the canoe to drift until its bow was against the base of a huge rock that formed the end of the bay, and he was again scrutinizing the shore line in an attempt to discover where the canoe had been drawn out when he noticed that the bow of his own craft was no longer against the base of the huge rock. It was slowly but surely drifting toward the mouth of the bay.

He paddled close to the rock, watching the current, and when the bow of the canoe struck a curtain of willows he was about to back-paddle when he caught a glimpse of water beyond them.

A stroke forward and he was through the willows. There was a triumphant grin on his face as he forced the canoe through still another curtain of willows and found himself on a smooth, dark stream at the bottom of a gorge.

The gorge was possibly twenty feet wide. Granite walls,

straight and tall, rose above him. A hundred feet or so ahead was an abrupt bend; the gorge ran straight north, till at a distance of perhaps half a mile the huge rock formation ended and the stream ran through an open section of country much like that through which he had been traveling for many days. And far away, perhaps a mile, he saw the canoe for which he had been searching. It was in a patch of sunlight, and the paddle was flashing rapidly.

It wasn't a trap; that was certain. For Blanche Devake was doing her best to escape him. He was puzzled now, but was determined to overtake her.

HIS CANOE was leaping through the lazy current. He expected that somewhere along the gorge stream, the woman would meet Blandin and Kelso. Sooner or later they would strike again, and he would rather meet them now, in the daylight, than have them dogging him through the wilderness, to creep upon him while he slept.

He gained upon the woman. Once, after he had paddled about a mile, he saw her pull her canoe from the stream and begin a portage. She was amazingly rapid in her movements, and she handled the canoe easily. He knew that he would have to work hard to overtake her.

When he reached the portage he drew the canoe up, tossed out the two packs—retaining nothing but his rifle, which he held in his right hand while carrying the canoe over the portage—and was soon sending the lightened craft forward with amazing speed.

He gained steadily, for his paddle dipped more frequently than the woman's, and his strokes were more powerful. The woman seemed to be tiring rapidly. She plied her paddle more slowly, at times splashing as though too weary to direct her strokes.

She presently reached a point where the water grew shallow, where great jagged rocks were strewn so thickly in the bed of the stream that a canoe could not be forced between them. She grounded the canoe.

To Fallon's amazement she did not attempt to make the portage, but leaped from the canoe and started to run into a level which stretched from a huge mound of rocks on the shore.

Fallon's canoe was beached almost as quickly as hers, for he had been only a hundred feet or so behind. He drove it high on the land, leaped out and ran with mighty strides around the mound of rocks behind which she had vanished.

As he reached the mound of rocks and had a clear view of what was beyond them, he halted abruptly.

Seated upon a small stone about a dozen yards from where he had stopped was the woman. Her face was flushed, her bosom was heaving rapidly. She had evidently pulled her stocking cap off, for it was lying on the ground at her feet, and her hair, long and abundant, had cascaded to her shoulders. It gleamed and glinted in the strong sunlight like strands of finely spun gold.

Beyond her, perhaps a hundred yards, was a bend in the stream where the portage ended. Beached on the sloping shore were half a dozen canoes. Half a dozen Indians, bearing caribou spears and belt-axes, were running toward the woman, gibbering excitedly.

Fallon stood, filled with sudden self-derision.

He had blundered, and was in for a fight. He was aware of an obscure embarrassment because of the mistake he had made, but he drew his feet together and glanced along the sights of the rifle he still carried.

The woman was not Blanche Devake.

She was younger. A girl. Certainly not more than twenty years old. And the savages who were running toward her were her friends. It was apparent that they had seen her as she came around the mound of rocks, breathless and terrorized, and that they were charging, intent upon protecting and avenging her.

CHAPTER IX

GAIL HAMMOND

FALLON'S RIFLE WAS rigid and his cheek was against the stock. He took aim at the chest of a giant Indian who had swiftly drawn ahead of the others in the run from the canoes to the woman. He followed the movements of the savage—yet he did not fire. There would still be time when the spearmen passed the woman, who was the object of their concern.

At the distance of a dozen yards he would be in danger of their spears, which he knew they hurled with a side motion that produced incredible speed; and yet he held his fire, hoping the woman would act to prevent the threatened clash.

There was wisdom in Fallon's decision. Even before the first savage reached her she was on her feet, facing the spearmen, holding up one hand commandingly and speaking to them sharply, in a language that Fallon did not understand.

He was amazed at the effect of her words. Some of the Indians halted so quickly that they went to their knees; while the largest of them—the one whose broad chest had been covered by Fallon's gun—threw himself backward and went down in a heap. His spear fell from his hand and he sat motionless, glaring.

She was a tall girl, taller than Blanche Devake. Her figure had a fullness, which suggested curves without emphasizing them; it indicated strength, and grace of movement. Her shoulders were broad but not masculine. This woman—this girl—was a personage.

She stood, coldly watching Fallon, with a commanding, authoritative, challenging gleam which would have embarrassed many men in Fallon's position.

Not Fallon. His gaze was never more steady than now, as he lowered his rifle and doffed his cap; and his admiration could not be concealed. This sturdy, graceful and regal young woman had stirred in him an emotion that he had never yet experienced.

It was not love at first sight. It was not desire. It was merely a strong man's admiration for one of nature's masterpieces.

She was beautiful, and the skin of her face and neck was satiny and flawless with the dusky peachbloom tint of perfect health. Yet it was not her visible charms that stirred him. It was something deeper and more substantial than these. It was the spirit he glimpsed—the sturdy, courageous heart of her. It shone from her eyes; he felt it in the poise of her lithe young body, in the set of her head. She was the spirit of the wilderness. Her beauty was the beauty of the animals that roam the forest trails.

But he was moved to silent mirth when, with a movement which was as unconscious as it was feminine, she reached up and brushed aside the mass of hair which the gusty wind had blown over her face. With several deft motions she caught it up, twisted it into various glistening ropes and coils, and tucked it in.

FALLON smiled. And Fallon's smile could be very tantalizing. It must have annoyed the girl, for she drew herself up haughtily and her eyes flashed angrily.

"You are amused," she said. Her voice concealed a taunt, and yet he knew that she was perplexed and curious. "Are you amused at my spearmen? Had I not halted them, you would not now be standing there, mocking."

"Not mocking you," returned Fallon with a gentleness that had always been his way with women. "Merely admiring you. I have looked upon many women, and perhaps not one has been as fair as you. And yet all have had the same feminine

habit of tucking in the stray wisps of hair. That is what brought
the smile, and nothing else."

"And why were you trying to catch me?"

"I am sorry for that. I thought you were another. When I
last saw her, she wore garments very like yours."

"Her name?"

"Blanche Devake."

"Is she your friend?"

The girl's eyes were now gleaming with disdain. She was
primitive and had not learned to conceal her passions, and so
Fallon knew the Devake woman was known and hated.

"I may safely name her among my enemies," said Fallon.

The girl gazed straight at him. He was conscious that he was
being probed and judged.

"What is your name, and what are you doing in this country?"
she asked.

He told her.

She caught her breath sharply, and trembled. As Fallon
watched her he saw a scarlet tide steal up her throat and spread
to her cheeks and forehead. Her eyes closed and she swayed.
Then the color receded. She stood now, gazing at Fallon fierce-
ly, her lithe young body rigid.

"How am I to know that you are telling the truth?"

"How do I know that you are not one of Lin's enemies?"
smiled Fallon. "Lin is alive. He was in this valley, and you have
talked with him. Perhaps you know where he is, and are holding
him for Blandin and the others."

"You know better than that, Fallon," she answered, straight-
ening proudly. "A moment ago I betrayed myself. I knew that
you had read my secret. Lin Underhill was here, in this valley.
He was hurt. I brought him back to health. I love him. I hate
Blandin and Kelso and the Devake woman, and if I had thought
that you were leagued with them against Lin my spearmen
would have killed you before now.

"You are a man, Fallon. You are strong, shrewd, brave. I saw that when you came around the corner of the rocks and saw my spearmen. You were surprised, but no panic overtook you; you even smiled as you laid your cheek against your rifle and aimed at Wattanooka's chest. You do not look at me as Blandin looked at me. And yet you may be Blandin's friend."

IN A POCKET of Fallon's shirt were the photograph of Lin Underhill and the note Lin had written to the guide, Jackwoon, on the day of his supposed death. These Fallon gave the girl.

After gazing long at the picture she suddenly hugged it to her breast.

"Yes, yes," she murmured, "it is Lin. And that is how Lin writes." Suddenly she grew cold again, and suspicious. "But why are you in this country without a guide? A stranger would get lost."

He told of his experiences since landing at Rossville.

"Yes," she finally said, nodding; "it is true. For early this morning from behind a clump of willows far up the river I saw you hurl a heavy rock through the bottom of a canoe. I saw Jackwoon sitting on a rock holding his wounded arm. And then I fled downstream. I paddled swiftly and was far ahead of you. But I lingered too long on the river and you saw me. Jackwoon has sold himself to Blandin and I did not think he could be your guide. But now I believe you. You must go with me to Mercie Valley. It is my home, and my mother's home. There I shall tell you how I came to know Lin Underhill, and Blandin and Kelso, and some others And after I have told you these things, you will still go on, because of me—because I want you to find Lin and bring him back to me."

"Yes," answered Fallon, "I shall go. But first I shall return to the last portage for my packs."

The girl quickly turned, clapped her hands and spoke to the squatting Indians. Instantly obeying her, they leaped to their feet, ran to the beach where their canoes lay, seized three of them, returned, trotting, to the open water above, launched their craft and sped away.

Fallon watched them for an instant. Then he turned to the girl.

"What is your name?" he asked.

"Gail Hammond."

"Your Indians love you, Gail," said Fallon.

"Yes," she answered, simply. "When they saw you standing there aiming your rifle at them they knew you could kill them all. And yet they would have willingly died, if I had said the word. Did you observe Wattanooka?"

"The biggest?"

Gail nodded.

"He is as big as you, Fallon. Perhaps he is as strong. He is proud of his strength. If you should do anything to hurt me—you or any other man—Wattanooka would never quit your trail until he had killed you. Twice he has begged me to let him search for Lin. He hates Blandin."

"Why don't you let him search for Lin?"

"He shall, now," said Gail. "He shall go with you."

CHAPTER X

MURDER IN THE WOODS

FALLON'S CANOE WAS portaged, his packs placed in it by the Indians, and, paddling steadily, he followed in the wake of the other canoes, northward. Gail Hammond, alone, was in the first canoe, followed by Wattanooka.

Shortly before the short twilight came on they were in camp for the night. Fallon estimated they had traveled at least twenty miles. The character of the country had changed very little. There were some vast, barren stretches, rolling and rocky; some low-growing timber; swamps; thickets of willow; some poplars. On various sloping ridges and swells was reindeer moss; here and there was a stretch of vivid color where the scarlet poppies reared their heads; and occasionally appeared the red *bakneesh;* and between the rocks on the ridges the white snow-flowers.

Flung against the skyline on all sides was the high rock wall that shut the valley from the outside world, a ragged, desolate rim grimly guarding this sunken garden spot.

Fallon rigged his canvas shelter against the north wind, built a small fire to keep the winged pests away, lit his pipe and smoked, watching his fire. Darkness grew upon them, although the white light of the north still glowed upon the horizon. He heard no step, no sound. Yet he sensed a presence and turned his head to see Gail kneeling at the end of his shelter.

In the glow of the firelight her face was calm and serious. Unsmilingly, she said:

"I'm coming in; I want to talk."

In this visit was no stealth, no embarrassment, no blushing to reveal consciousness of sex; no apologetic smiling. In her manner was only naturalness and dignity which needed no words to manifest it. She got into the shelter with him, crossed her hands over her knees, and sighed deeply.

"I've been bothered, thinking about Lin," she said, then frankly studied his face for some minutes before she again spoke.

"Tell me why Lin's father chose you to search for him."

Fallon told her that he had never inquired about that. He had got a telegram from the elder Underhill which had opened negotiations. He had come because he had wanted to come and because he had had nothing else to do at the time.

"Some one had told him about you? To be talked about that way, you must have done something to make people talk."

"Oh, people will talk."

"Yes; if you do something bad. And they won't talk about you if you are only just ordinarily good. But if you have done something very good they will talk about you. What had you done to make them talk about you?"

"Nothing. I had just lived like other people."

She shook her head at the fire.

"You've done things, but you are too modest to talk about them," she said. "But of course you couldn't be boastful and brave at the same time. You are a brave man, and you would like Lin if you should meet him. For Lin is a brave man, too."

She sat silent, gazing at the fire. Her firm young face had lines in it now as she strove with her thoughts and her problems. The stars came out, glittering like gems in the dusky velvet blue of the sky, and the solemn shadows of the forest grew darker and more mysterious. And then, without preface or further delay, she told the story of Lin Underhill's visit to the valley.

"There will be no sense in what I am going to tell you unless I begin at the beginning," she said.

And this is how, afterward, Fallon remembered it:

ADAM HAMMOND—Gail's father—and a man named Lumly Randall, had come into the Hudson Bay country twenty-five years ago. They had taken ship from Quebec and had disembarked at Churchill, where they had outfitted for a trip inland. Lumly Randall was a rich man. He had told Adam Hammond that his trip to the Hudson Bay country was to be for the purpose of entering the fur trade in opposition to the Hudson's Bay Company. That enterprise might be hazardous, but Randall intimated that he would have plenty of influential men behind him if it came to a fight with the established company.

Randall built himself a house in the wilderness north of the Fox River. It was an enormous structure of stones that were to be picked up all over the face of the country. There were twenty rooms, secret tunnels and passages, a tower. The doors were constructed of stout timbers swung on heavy iron hinges and firmly barred; the windows were shuttered with heavy planks.

In the stuff that Randall had brought with him—half a ship's cargo, Adam Hammond had said—were two small cannon, some fowling pieces, two dozen rifles of heavy caliber; some great, long pistols and several of more modern pattern; cutlasses, swords, pikes, and axes. A barrel of gunpowder had been freighted up the river along with the arms.

Adam Hammond had made some remark about these warlike implements, but Randall, a great hulking man of thirty at that time, with one eye—the left—missing, had laughed and kept his silence.

The great house was built, and occupied by Randall. Later, when Randall took a squaw to live with him—a Cree woman whom he bought from the chief of a nomadic tribe—Hammond left him. Indeed, by this time Hammond began to suspect that Randall was something more than a rich man; he began to believe that Randall was a man with a price upon his head. He had made a fortress of the stone house, and his conduct while in it was not that of a man who had been reared a gentleman.

There were riotous doings there; much drinking and gambling, and the gamblers and drinkers were not the hunters and trappers of the section, nor were they men from the factor's house at Churchill. They were men who drifted in from the outside, from Churchill mostly, and judging from their talk and actions they were seafaring men who had known Randall in his earlier days.

Once a woman and a child appeared there. The woman was delicate and thin, emaciated as if by some wasting disease, with dark hollows under her eyes. The child was a girl about two or three years of age—a pretty thing with dark hair and eyes and a disconcerting habit of staring at one.

Hammond had not told Gail what had happened in the big house; he had related no details. But in the main she had gathered that what went on there was wicked enough. And as Hammond had no liking for those things, and as Randall showed no disposition to set about the work of founding a trading post, Hammond left him. Randall laughed at him, but let him go because there had been no definite agreement between them.

Randall had grown disgustingly vulgar and bestial, and it was with great relief that Hammond went his separate way. He went westward into the wilderness, built himself a cabin, and devoted his time to trapping. He prospered at this and sold his furs to the factor at Churchill. Later he met a girl at the trading post, and in the course of time the girl became Hammond's wife, and Gail's mother.

HAMMOND kept working his way westward. While running his trap lines he prospected a little, and at last on one of his trips into the western wilderness he found this valley. It was a paradise. Hammond had accidentally found a secret entrance to it. He built another cabin and settled his wife, now a mother, in it.

He had found the valley inhabited by a tribe of Indians, with whom he had made friends. The Indians were Chippewas who had sought independence from a chief who was offensive to them. They had found the valley, and for several years they had lived in it without the knowledge of the remainder of the tribe. Most of the Indians living in the valley had known Hammond's wife while she had served the factor at Churchill. They liked and trusted her, and they liked and trusted Adam Hammond. In time they began to look upon him as their leader, and they renounced their tribal rituals and adopted Hammond's God.

They had lived peaceably for several years. And then Hammond, prospecting in the valley, had found gold—free gold in staggering quantity.

Hammond had taken some of the gold to Churchill to have it assayed, and somehow the news got to Randall. Randall swore that he would have half of the golden treasure because it was he who had brought Adam Hammond to the country, and furthermore between them was a written agreement to the effect that he and Hammond were to share together in all things that they might find.

But Randall was not able to find Hammond. Word of Randall's ragings had reached Hammond. And so he took no more gold to Churchill or anywhere else. He left it where he had found it, in the valley. And there it had remained until this day.

But Hammond had made one mistake. He had not told his wife or daughter where he had found the gold, and he had left with them no diagram or map of the section in which he had found it. He had kept the secret to himself.

And then one day he had set out for Rossville to get some supplies. Wattanooka had gone with him. They had been absent several days, when one morning Wattanooka returned, alone. He was paddling his canoe with one arm—the other was broken, the hand smashed. There were wounds all over his body, and a great gash on the top of his head where he had evidently been struck with some heavy weapon.

In the bottom of the canoe was a strange white man who later identified himself as Linton Underhill. Underhill was unconscious and used up about as badly as Wattanooka. Adam Hammond had been killed.

LATER, Wattanooka told the story. He had reached a place called "Big Tree" portage on the way to Rossville. Wattanooka was carrying the canoe and Hammond was behind him, with a light pack. In a spot where there was some dense undergrowth he heard Hammond call out sharply. He dropped the canoe and turned, to see Hammond struggling with half a dozen men—whites and Indians.

Wattanooka leaped forward to help Hammond, and was met by a spear-thrust from the brush. From another point he received a second spear or an arrow, and then others—he did not know how many. Then a blow on the top of the head, and he knew nothing more until he awakened to see a number of Indians and white men sitting in a circle around Hammond.

The white men were Blandin, Kelso, a big, evil-eyed stranger who was called Revella, and Lin Underhill. It was the first time that Wattanooka had seen any of the men, but while lying there motionless and conscious, he had heard all their names spoken. He had identified them, one after the other, for there were thoughts of vengeance in his heart.

Underhill and Hammond were bound. Jackwoon was there, among the Indians. The Indians were silent, while the white men talked. The white men were questioning Hammond about his gold. And Hammond would not answer.

They tortured Hammond. They placed glowing embers upon his arms and legs and sat there grinning cruelly as the coals seared Hammond's flesh. They prodded him with spears and arrows and inflicted unmentionable cruelties upon him.

But Hammond would not talk. Wattanooka had no power over his muscles. They would not respond to his will. He was forced to lie there and listen.

After a while the white men left Hammond. They went away in canoes, leaving the Indians to guard Hammond. They were gone a long time, and while they were away Hammond, who had fainted, regained consciousness and talked with Lin Underhill. Wattanooka overheard them.

Hammond asked Underhill many questions. Hammond told Underhill about his wife and daughter, about the hidden valley, how to find the entrance to it, and about the gold—where it would be found. He got Underhill to promise that he would find the valley, apprise his wife and daughter of what had happened to him, and tell them about the gold. He thought Wattanooka was dead. But Wattanooka was not dead. He could not talk or move. Only his ears had been awake, he said.

Hammond told Underhill that he had received a death wound. A spear had bitten him more deeply than had been intended. He could feel his life going.

When Hammond's captors returned Hammond was dead. There was a great deal of cursing, and in a fury his body was thrown into the brush to be devoured by wolves.

The white men released Underhill. Blandin and Revella, standing near Underhill, laughed and told him to take Jackwoon and resume his travels. It appeared to Wattanooka that Underhill and Jackwoon must have accidentally come upon Blandin and his crew just as Hammond had been attacked, or just after.

Underhill told Blandin and Revella that he would be glad to part from such company. Blandin and Revella continued to laugh at Underhill. They were near to blows, though, for Underhill's contempt was strong and his words were bitter. He called to Jackwoon, turned his back to Blandin and Revella and began to walk away.

Then Blandin and Revella shot him, in the back. Both took deliberate aim with their pistols. Underhill fell, face down. Revella walked to him, kicked him several times in the side and the face, and left him. They all went away then, leaving Hammond and Underhill and Wattanooka for dead.

WATTANOOKA did not die, though for two or three days it seemed he would. Nor did Underhill die.

Here Wattanooka had boasted a little to Gail Hammond. His pride in himself was excusable, though, for never had she seen a man more terribly wounded.

Consider, she told Fallon: Wattanooka's body bore a dozen wounds. His left arm was broken. The hand was smashed. They found three deep spear wounds in him, together with half a dozen knife and arrow wounds. He had managed to bury Hammond, he had kept Underhill from dying; he had got Underhill into his canoe and had paddled all that distance with one good arm.

Wattanooka was a strong man. He was the strongest man in the country. His strength was acknowledged and he was proud of it.

But he had almost been retaken by the two white men, Revella and Blandin. He had traveled by night, fearing to meet the white men again, and one night while slipping down the river in his canoe he had seen a camp fire on an island: had paddled his canoe gently into some willows and had heard the white men talking. They had been told by one of the Indians— who understood a little English—that Hammond had talked to Underhill about the gold; and they were going back to the scene of the tragedy in the hope of finding Underhill still alive. If he was still living it was their plan to restore him to health and make him talk.

They had not succeeded in finding Underhill then, of course, but they must have suspected that both he and Wattanooka had survived and escaped, for their bodies were not where they had been left. And finally, while Underhill was regaining his strength, word reached Gail that they had found Hammond's grave and that they knew Wattanooka and Underhill had escaped them.

And then, after Underhill recovered and became strong again, he decided to complete his work, and with Wattanooka to guide him he again set out to explore the wilderness. And one day after Wattanooka had returned to camp from a hunt he found the camp wrecked and Underhill gone. He trailed Underhill for several days.

Underhill had been captured by a large party of Indians and white men. Once he had seen Underhill; but had not been able to rescue him, for there had been too many in the party and Underhill had been too well guarded. He had lurked near, however, and had seen Underhill taken to Randall's stone house. He had even approached the house several times, hoping for an opportunity to get near Underhill, but the great stone walls and the forbidding atmosphere of the place had awed him and he had returned to the valley, bearing his ill news.

"**WATTANOOKA** is not afraid of men," Gail concluded. "He is afraid of things he does not understand."

"How long is it since Lin disappeared?" asked Fallon.

"That was six months ago. It was in the winter. But there was a thaw, and Lin was restless. He wished to go out in the spring."

"He told you where the gold might be found?"

"Yes. I have seen the place."

She clasped her hands over her knees and gazed into the fire, which had burned low. Fallon sat, steadily puffing at his pipe.

"Do you think Lin is still alive?" asked Fallon.

"Yes. He is alive. And he has not told them where they may find the gold."

"How do you know that?"

Gail touched her breast. "Something here tells me he is still alive," she said. "And if he had told them where to find the gold they would have come here to get it," she added. "For they know about the secret entrance to the valley—the one that father found when he came here. And, too, I saw Blanche Devake and Blandin at the water entrance. They would come and search for the gold but they are afraid of my Indians and the search would take too long. While they were searching, Wattanooka and my Indians would kill them."

The darkness had grown intense and Fallon's fire had gone out. He and the girl sat for a long time, saying nothing. Then she bade him good night, and moved away in the darkness.

Almost instantly, he heard her voice, a few feet from his shelter.

"Wattanooka!" she exclaimed. "What are you doing here?"

There was amazement in her voice, and stern accusation. It was apparent to Fallon that she was indignant over finding the Indian so close to his shelter; she had not given him orders to spy upon the white man.

"Me come watch," explained Wattanooka. His voice was sullen, but respectful. "No like white man. Come see no hurt Gail."

The girl laughed, and went on, taking the Indian with her.

So Wattanooka was an enemy. Fallon only smiled as he stretched himself on his bed of pine boughs.

CHAPTER XI

MAN TO MAN

AT DAWN THE next morning Fallon emerged from his shelter, leaped into his canoe and paddled half a mile down the stream to a wide, deep spot which was an ideal place for a swim.

There had been no movement at the camp, no fires.

He laid his clothes carefully upon a bowlder near the edge, and plunged in. The water was warmer than the frosty air, and he swam a while, then floated, lying on his back.

He turned over to swim back into deeper water—and observed that he had company.

Wattanooka had driven his canoe into the pool while Fallon had been idly floating on his back. He had beached the canoe, and at the moment Fallon became aware of him he was standing on the sandy beach removing his knee-length deerskin trousers—the only garment he wore, besides his moccasins.

Wattanooka was magnificently proportioned. His muscles were long, smooth, and were laid in a rippling sheath all over his body, except at the stomach where they formed two low, flat ridges. As he stood upon the beach, naked, he looked like a figure that had been carved out of red granite by a master. For a savage, he was handsome.

He did not look at Fallon. And he seemed to know the pool, for he dived into it and disappeared, to emerge as noiselessly as a seal, with his sullen black eyes upon Fallon.

Remembering that Wattanooka had told Gail he did not

like him, Fallon kept a watchful eye upon the Indian, though he pretended to ignore him, and did not cut short his swim.

When Fallon, refreshed and reinvigorated, finally swam to the sloping beach and stood erect in the shallow water, Wattanooka was no less obvious in his admiration of the white man's physique, as he followed him ashore.

For Fallon was a perfect match for the savage. Standing side by side the Indian would have been taller than Fallon, but the white man's muscles were as clearly defined, his shoulders were as broad, and his strength was quite as apparent.

Yet there was something more in Fallon—something that Wattanooka lacked. Of the two nude men who were now facing each other in this primitive environment, one carried in his heart the invincible courage and determination of a long line of conquerors; while the other, equally strong, was a son of a race whose fathers had met defeat after defeat in the long-drawn battle for possession of the frontiers.

FALLON had finally become convinced that Wattanooka's interest in him was hatred. And he was never the man to postpone an inevitable clash.

"Wattanooka," he said, "you followed me."

The Indian folded his great arms over his chest and spoke slowly.

"Gail tell white man much. White man say little. Wattanooka Gail's friend. What white man want here?"

In the Indian's eyes something besides hatred was glowing. Loyalty to his mistress was there, and determination, together with a certain wistfulness. A blending of many emotions. Interpreted by Fallon, the look meant that if Fallon's errand to the country was one of friendliness to Gail Hammond there could be no hatred between the two men, but if Fallon meant harm to the girl there must be a definite settlement now. One or the other would stay at the pool.

Fallon studied the Indian. He was reluctant to concede that

Wattanooka had any right to question him. But the fine loyalty of the savage to his mistress impressed him; and he smiled.

"White man came here to help Gail Hammond find Lin Underhill," he said. "That is all. White man will talk no more to Wattanooka."

The Indian's eyes flashed. His lips curved into a smile of friendliness. His great chest swelled. He extended his right hand in the white man's greeting, and after an instant Fallon seized it, gripping it firmly.

They stood there for an instant longer, searching each other's eyes while they tightened the bond between them.

"You strong," said the Indian. "Wattanooka strongest man in country," he added.

Primitive pride such as this Fallon had met before. Pride of strength had once been strong in him, and even now Wattanooka's boast touched him.

"Wattanooka speaks loudly. If Wattanooka's muscles are as strong as his voice he is a great man."

The Indian smiled confidently, and motioned Fallon to wrestle. There was no word between them as they moved about in the shallow water, then, feinting for holds, onto the sandy beach. There, chest to chest, they stood erect, their arms locked, each seeking to force the other to take a backward step. This was Wattanooka's idea of victory. Fallon understood. His feet sank into the sand, but they went no deeper than Wattanooka's. The great muscles of his back and thighs grew and expanded into rock-like ridges as he braced himself, and once his shoulders began to bulge backward from the strain.

Then the rock-like muscles began to writhe and squirm under the white skin. They grew knotted; they crawled into bunches around his shoulder blades, along his neck, down his thighs and at his hips. Slowly he straightened the red giant until the latter's body was almost perpendicular. Wattanooka's feet began to slide in the sand.

Fallon now resorted to science. He had tested Wattanooka's

strength and found it to be great, though not as great as his own. And now, to end the contest, he turned swiftly sideways to the red man, locked one of his arms under his own, swiftly bent his own body forward and threw Wattanooka a dozen feet out into the stream, into the deep water.

WATTANOOKA landed on his back, and the water splashed high as he vanished. Fallon got one look at his face as it disappeared beneath the surface, and saw amazement and chagrin depicted there. He was prepared to see the Indian emerge in a fighting rage; but when Wattanooka's face quickly appeared it was wreathed in a smile.

There was no rage in him, but only embarrassment. His boast of strength had not been vindicated. But he offered no excuse.

"You strong," he said. "Maybe stronger than Wattanooka. Know trick that Wattanooka not know. Look!"

And now he devised another test of strength. He dragged the two canoes into the water and lashed their noses together with a rope.

Fallon had played this game, also. With the bows of the canoes locked the two contestants were to paddle until one forced the other backward to a distance far enough to determine supremacy. Skill as well as strength would be needed to determine the winner of the paddling contest.

They manipulated the canoes to the center of the stream, and poised their paddles until Wattanooka gave a signal.

Their muscles swelled and leaped, and the water of the pool churned and foamed in a fury of agitation. Around and around went the canoes, their prows creaking and groaning as they clashed together; and for a quarter of an hour they strove with no apparent advantage to either. But at last Fallon's canoe began to move backward.

Realizing his defeat, Fallon did the graceful thing. He suddenly lifted his paddle aloft in token of surrender, and raised his voice full-throatedly in a cry of admiration for Wattanooka's skill and strength.

The Indian immediately ceased paddling, and leaned forward, his somberness gone, his teeth flashing in a broad smile. And yet for a time they said nothing more, for both were weary from their mighty efforts. At last Wattanooka spoke.

"You good man," he said, panting. "You stronger than Wattanooka. I win because I know trick with paddle."

"We are even there," laughed Fallon. "For I know some wrestling tricks."

The Indian shook his head, and his black eyes gleamed again.

"You fair," he said. "You win wrestling without trick. I feel you stronger."

There was respect in the Indian's eyes as they dressed, and Wattanooka related the story of Adam Hammond's death. It was evident that Blandin and Kelso, and the other man, Revella, were fiends.

Wattanooka's eyes burned with rage as he finished the tale and sat there looking at Fallon. "You go alone to stone house?"

Fallon grinned.

"Wattanooka is like the fox," he said. "He did not come to the pool to talk big, but to show his strength so that Fallon would take him to the stone house. Well—you go."

The Indian's chest swelled with pride, but he sat motionless otherwise, evidently restraining himself. But there was now no mistaking the expression in his eyes as he looked at the white man—they were worshipful.

CHAPTER XII

THE HIDDEN VALLEY

AN HOUR AFTER dawn the little fleet of canoes was again headed northward. Gail Hammond led the way, with the others trailing her. Fallon's canoe was directly behind Gail's with Wattanooka's close. Wherever the width of the stream permitted, the giant Indian would force his canoe alongside, to tell Fallon various things about the valley.

Wattanooka was intelligent. His knowledge of English had been imparted to him by Hammond, and then by Gail. She was "White Bird" to Wattanooka and the other members of the tribe. He was the nominal chief, but the actual authority was vested in Gail since the death of her father. The Indians worshipped her.

Adam Hammond had brought some books with him into the valley, and he had sent outside for others. Between Hammond and his wife and the books Gail had acquired an education. Her quick mind, absorbing the verbal pictures of history and fiction, had built a fanciful structure of conduct and manners which answered well. But her primitive frankness was sometimes devastating.

Late that afternoon they paddled out of the stream into a small lake, a mile and a half long and perhaps half as wide. It was in the center of a gently sloping country that stretched away from it for several miles to the north and the east and the west; and where the sloping land ended were the high and massive barriers of natural rock and bald and forbidding mountain peaks that isolated the valley from the outside world.

Yet the valley was a paradise, with fields of grain in abundance despite the shortness of the growing season. And even its winters were not as severe as in the higher land that encompassed it, for the high rock barrier formed a windbreak which shunted the wild storms upward.

On the north bank of the lake, sheltered by a gigantic rock overhang that swept outward in a huge arc, for more than a hundred feet, were a number of orderly log cabins inhabited by the Indians.

At the eastern end of the lake was the large Hammond cabin, a stone chimney sticking above the center of the gable roof. There were several smaller buildings behind the cabin.

The Indians, under the direction of Wattanooka, unloaded the canoes, carried the packs to the porch of the cabin and silently vanished into their own houses. Soon Fallon was on the porch, being presented to Mrs. Hammond.

Adam Hammond's widow was a small woman, almost slight. But there was a patient steadiness in her eyes and a quiet indomitability in her manner that Fallon knew was characteristic of women of the wilderness. They were fully aware of the hazards they faced, yet they were not afraid.

And now Gail went into the house. Presently they heard her voice at a distance. Apparently she was talking with one of the Indians.

MRS. HAMMOND had motioned Fallon to a chair and sat facing him. At the sound of Gail's voice she said, slowly:

"Gail is a beautiful girl."

"I have seen none more beautiful."

"She loves Lin Underhill. He is not as tall as you," said Mrs. Hammond. "Nor as broad. Nor is there in him the romance that there is in your appearance. You have seen a great deal of life, young man; and it has not spoiled you. You are an adventurer. The wild passions are in you, but they are governed by high ideals. Yet when you want a woman you will take her. Do you want Gail?"

"I do not want Gail," answered Fallon, steadily meeting her eyes.

"Then Gail is safe. If you wanted her I should be afraid for her."

Quietly, gently, she led him to talk about himself. And she, won by Fallon's simple directness, gave to him the story of her life in this wild country.

Lumly Randall, she said, was a former pirate. With men as bloodthirsty as himself, he had roamed the southern seas. There were stories of women captured by Randall, of men forced to walk the plank, of captives borne to distant lands and sold into slavery. All these tales were true, she assured Fallon, for she had sat many nights in the store room of the factor's building at Churchill and listened to them.

The wonder of it was that Randall was not apprehended. But, she had heard him boast that there were none who dared to turn him over to the law, for he knew things about men in high places that would convict them of guilt as great as his own.

And the telling of these things stirred Fallon greatly. For it seemed that beckoning to him were romance and danger and high adventure such as he had not yet encountered.

CHAPTER XIII

THROUGH THE BARRIER

ON THE MORNING of the third day following his appearance at the Hammond home, Fallon and Wattanooka entered the evergreen forest at the rear of the cabin. Mrs. Hammond and Gail watched them go.

The Indian preceded Fallon into the evergreens, for they were going out of the valley through the secret passage that would lead them directly into the wild country in which the stone house was situated, and Wattanooka knew the trail.

There was no trail that Fallon could see, and yet Wattanooka strode ahead confidently, holding a northeasterly direction. No man could follow it unless he had threaded it before, and Wattanooka charged Fallon to mark carefully the various rock formations in case he had to return alone.

Fallon and the Indian were traveling light. The canoes had been left behind. Upon Fallon's back was a light pack containing his canvas shelter, a small store of provisions and a few cooking utensils. In his pockets were a number of cartridges for the rifle he carried, and for the .45 Colt in the holster at his right hip. Around him was a cartridge belt studded with other cartridges.

Wattanooka likewise carried a small pack and a rifle. He carried no revolver. At his belt was a long, ivory-hafted *kiliutok* knife and behind him a fluted belt-ax. His only clothes were the deerskin trousers, and a pair of moose-hide moccasins.

They were many hours getting through the forest. But at last the trees thinned out and they began to thread a section in which great rocks and bowlders seemed to have been thrown by some mighty power.

Wattanooka slipped swiftly between and around the gigantic rocks until he found a channel that appeared to be of natural construction. At first it was only a few feet deep, but as the Indian continued to follow it the rock walls beside it grew higher, and the channel deeper, until it became a chasm with perpendicular sides. Then it angled, and they were smothered with an impenetrable darkness.

They were more than an hour in traversing the dark passageway. Wattanooka kept guiding Fallon with his voice, and Fallon kept close to him. And after a while the darkness lifted a little and a beam of light far in front of them indicated that they were approaching an outlet. When they finally stood in the open, blinking against the white light of the morning, they were through the high rock barrier which rimmed the valley, but were in a desolate, rocky section beyond which was still another barrier.

WATTANOOKA found another channel through the confusion of rocks. The second barrier was not so thick as the first, but they were longer getting through it, because there was no subterranean passage to take them, and they were forced to thread narrow ledges that angled here and there through breaks in the rock wall, and into crevasses where there was no footing and they had to suspend their weight on their arms and hands or brace their feet against the sides.

They descended gradually until they were again at the base of the barrier. Dusk found them deep into the virgin timber. "This Cree country," warned Wattanooka. "Maybe they here, maybe not here. Who can tell?"

They were up at dawn the following morning, and emerged from the timber onto a great stretch of barren country, where granite mounds reached to the horizon, like small rolling swells on an ocean. The pair, two atoms moving across the surface of a dead planet, toiled onward all that day and the next, to find themselves at last in another belt of virgin timber.

It was just at sundown of the fourth day that the two reached the farther edge of this forest, and cautiously approached the banks of a small river where, from the concealment of a dense growth of willows, they could see Randall's mysterious stone castle.

CHAPTER XIV

A PIRATE'S WELCOME

RANDALL'S HOUSE STOOD upon a ridge of rock, for here and there were bare, smooth spots where the naked granite was exposed. The ridge sloped gently downward to the stream at the point where Fallon and Wattanooka were concealed, but east and west the slope grew gradually sharper until it descended almost perpendicularly into the water. Directly behind the house the ridge was timbered, and it ran, broad and vast, into the northern distance. East and west of the ridge were muskeg belts; then more timber and ridges that wandered away into the horizon.

The house faced southward. It was a great, long, gloomy structure, as massive and forbidding as a medieval fortress. It lacked the parapet walls, the bastioned towers, the moats and the drawbridges, but its huge rock walls, its planked doorways and its timber-shuttered windows suggested that its builder had had some thought of defense.

The roof was flat. And now, giving more attention to the details of the building, Fallon discovered that there were two towers, after all. They were on the rear corners, above the heavy coping of the second story, and he could see their roofs running up to the peaks that were only just visible against the green background of the trees.

Despite the fact that the house was located in the wilderness there was about it an atmosphere that was distinctly of the sea and of seafaring people. Directly in front of what appeared to be the main entrance to the house, and upon a huge granite block which stood on a broad rock level in front of the doorway was a ship's binnacle. The instrument was made of brass and was polished until it glittered even in the dusk; while at the western corner of the house, on another rock level, was a ship's wheel, brightly painted.

About halfway down the slope was a small cedar pole, painted and polished, rigged with ropes and pulleys for a flag. There was no flag on it now, and Fallon smilingly reflected that if one had been there, it should have been black.

In spite of the gloomy, forbidding atmosphere of the place there was an air of neatness about it. The glass windows were spotless, and the little wharf across the stream from them was clean as the freshly-scrubbed deck of a ship.

The big front door was open. It swung inward and was constructed of wood which was varnished and polished until it shone like glass. There was a small barred opening near the top.

The outside door, which was swung back against the house and fastened with a great iron hook, was made of solid planking. Its massive iron hinges were visible at the butts, as was the huge elbow hasp with which it was fastened when closed. The windows, too, were equipped with shutters of like material.

It was strange, to find this house in the wilderness, and yet it was as primitive as its surroundings. Having stood on its rocky eminence for a quarter of a century, its rugged rock walls were dark, and the chinks between the rocks were green with a rich moss.

Off to the east side of the house, at a little distance back in the timber, were the huts of an Indian village. Fallon and Wattanooka could make out dark forms of the Crees moving here and there in the semi-gloom of the trees. The village was near the river—which doubled northward at that point—and on the beach were a number of canoes.

IN FRONT of the house, west of the doorway, were several stout chairs, and in three of the chairs sat men. Nearest the door was Randall. Fallon easily identified him because of the leather patch over his left eye, and from his stature and his brutish appearance.

His shoulders were so broad that they projected beyond the large chair's back, his arms dangled over its sides.

His head was large, but its greatest circumference was at a line that would be at his eyebrows and just above his ears. Below that, in the back, was a mass of solid flesh, like gristle, which formed the back of his neck and ran around under his ears to form jaws that resembled the jowls of a hog. His chin, however, was the chin of a bulldog, and one would be at a loss as to which animal he resembled most. Perhaps one would choose the beast that one detested most.

Lumly Randall's head was almost all below his eyebrows and his ears. What little there was of it above those points was insignificant insofar as it affected his appearance. His body was big, but not fat. It appeared to be sheathed with muscle rather than excess flesh.

The man seated next to him at his right was tall, slender and dark. His nose was long and full, making his short upper lip seem still shorter in contrast. His lower lip drooped at the center with a sensual fullness. His chin was pointed and prominent and his eyes deep-set under heavy, black brows.

He was a well-built man, lithe and muscular, with an alertness that was physical rather than mental. Like Lumly Randall, he was an animal, but he was sleek and neat in his habits. Fallon could tell from his mannerisms. He flecked dust from his clothing with his handkerchief; he straightened his tie a number of times; occasionally he stroked his black hair as if making certain it was lying just right; and half a dozen times while Fallon watched him he drew out a small glass and surveyed his reflection.

"Revella," whispered Wattanooka. "The man who look in glass. What he see to make him look? Maybe Wattanooka bust face off bimeby."

"What do you want here?" demanded Randall.

"The big one is Randall?"

"Um. Fat. Like beaver. Big eat. Big drink."

The third man was thick and short. Except that his features were large, the face was not one to arrest a glance. The man was colorless and accustomed to taking orders, for he was continually leaning toward the other two, nodding his head, listening, not being listened to when he spoke.

"Know him?" asked Fallon.

Wattanooka shook his head negatively.

"Him 'come-along-too,'" he said with contempt. "Him no good."

Mosquitoes must have bothered the men, for they went indoors, closing the inner door behind them. Not long after that a light flared and the dancing beams of a kerosene lamp illuminated the windows of the room which the men had entered. The rest of the house was dark.

And now there occurred a singular thing, a thing that made Fallon rub his eyes in an effort to banish an illusion that suddenly seized him—the illusion that he was in reality looking

at a medieval fortress. For from out of the darkness behind the
house came two men. They wore baldrics from which were
suspended broad-bladed swords, and they bore halberds with
long shafts and broad, long heads. The curved axes and the
heads themselves were of sharp, polished steel.

The men were sentries, taking their stations for the night.
Each patrolled two sides of the castle, returning to meet again
at the point from which they started. They walked with the
peculiar, rolling gait of seafaring men. Both were short men
and they looked rather ridiculous in their rigging.

Fallon asked Wattanooka if the men had been there when
Wattanooka had previously visited the stone house.

"No there," said the Indian. "Lot sailor man. No soldier."

Lumly Randall feared something. What it was did not
concern Fallon at this instant. He had come here to enter the
stone house to search for Lin Underhill, and he was merely
deciding how to proceed.

Now, with darkness coming, he talked long and earnestly
with Wattanooka, perfecting plans and arranging signals. Wattanooka was to stay outside. He was to watch the windows for
the signals. If opportunity came during the day or night, they
would meet far back in the forest, at a designated place.

Wattanooka remained in the willows while Fallon slipped
out of them and entered the timber, to emerge upon the bank
of the river at a little distance. He still bore a light pack, his
Colt and his rifle.

HE STEPPED boldly out of the timber and walked along the
bank, searching for a shallow where he might cross. When he
found it he leaped lightly from stone to stone, succeeding in
crossing without wetting his moccasins; and made his way up
the bank to the stone slope in front of the house. One of the
sentries had seen him. His halberd was grounded with a re-
sounding crash, he was erect and rigid.

"Avast there!" he said. "What do you want?"

Fallon pretended to be startled. Then he grinned at the man.

"Man, you look like a page out of a picture book!" he said. "How did you get here?"

"You'll know soon enough if you don't say what you want," growled the man with a strong cockney accent.

"Is this the way Randall tells you to greet his guests?" returned Fallon.

"A guest, are you? Well, that's different. We got orders an' they must be obeyed." He lifted a hand in salute, stepped to the door and rapped upon it peculiarly.

It was opened almost instantly by Lumly Randall who, Fallon surmised, had been close to it from the beginning of the conversation with the guard. A pistol was in Randall's right hand, and he peered with suspicion and hostility at his visitor in the last remnants of the fading light.

"What do you want?" he asked gruffly. "This is no tavern!"

"Are you Lumly Randall?"

"Yes."

"Then I'm right," said Fallon. He began to unsling his pack and it dropped with a light, sodden thud to the great rock platform just outside the doorway. "Lumly Randall was the name. A stone house. I'm Jim Fallon."

Randall's lips curved with cold contempt and his bulldog chin began to move outward.

"You're Jim Fallon, eh?" he said. "Well, that name don't mean anything to me. So you'd best slip your anchor and drift away from here."

"All right. Blandin must have directed me wrong."

Fallon turned, swung his pack upward and began to slip into the straps. He was turning away when Randall's voice halted him.

"Blandin, you say? Blandin sent you? Well, why in hell didn't you say that in the first place?"

"Blandin told me you'd be expecting me."

"He did, eh? When did he tell you that?"

"At Rossville. Two weeks ago, I'd met him at Grand Marias, where he'd told me to meet him."

Randall was peering intently at Fallon, trying to see his face in the dim light. Now he stepped back and gruffly invited Fallon inside, "To see what you look like."

Apparently his inspection of Fallon left him still perturbed and uncertain, for in the flickering light of the oil lamp in a wall bracket Randall's good eye was still hostile and suspicious.

With his pack still on his back Fallon stepped inside. Again he slipped out of the straps and permitted the pack to drop. Then he straightened and stretched himself as though to relax his muscles. Saying nothing, Randall stepped back a little and watched him. The pistol was still in Randall's hand.

FALLON found himself in a big room. At first glance he estimated its length at fifty feet and its width at thirty. In the center of the room between two huge stone columns was a long table upon which was a gilded cloth, with glasses and bottles on it. Revella and the other man sat there, silently watchful.

The room had a stone floor, made of great slabs which had been inaccurately smoothed and jointed, so that the surface was uneven. The chinks between the slabs were cemented and the entire floor was spotlessly clean. The two massive stone columns supported a massive beam ceiling.

On the further side of the room was a gigantic stone fireplace, with a great square breast which was recessed at about the height of a man's shoulder into a wide mantel shelf. Above the mantel shelf was an enormous moose-head. The head had been prepared by a clever hand, and the great horns were polished until they glistened.

On the mantel shelf was a small ship, full-rigged, with all its canvas set. It was flying a black flag which was adorned with skull and crossbones. The remaining space on the mantel was occupied by nautical miscellany—a stone tankard, a long-stemmed pipe, a sea glass, a cutlass, a clock, a pair of pistols with silver filigree work on their stocks.

At the end of the room, eastward was a great, brass-bound sea chest with dents in its sides and top. There were some marine pictures on the walls, and the walls themselves were painted. Several huge chairs were scattered about.

And now, standing there facing Lumly Randall it occurred to Fallon that even if he had not been informed of the ill repute of the big stone house he would not have failed to feel its evil atmosphere.

In this room there was a strange odor that paint could not dissipate, that cleanliness could not eliminate. It was a cloying odor, musty and clinging and persistent, though slight and faint like the breath of the sea that steals inland. Fallon had encountered the odor twice in his life, and each time the blood of murdered men had caused it.

Lumly Randall was now standing with his feet spread far apart. His huge legs were like posts; he was slouched forward a little and his big chin was on his chest as he regarded Fallon searchingly with his one eye.

"Blandin sent you here, eh?" he said. "What did he tell you he wanted you to do here?"

"That is between me and Blandin."

"What's holding Blandin at Rossville?"

"Blanche."

"Blanche who?"

"Devake. She took sick, bad. I don't know what it is. Landieu is taking care of her. It looked like she would be held up there a long time. So Blandin told me to take Jackwoon and come on. He said I might be doing some good instead of loafing there."

"What did he mean by saying you might do some good?"

"I don't know. I was to come here. I supposed you would know."

"Where's Jackwoon?"

"Jackwoon went back to Rossville. He brought me to the game trail on the Hayes directly south of here and told me to keep heading north. He thought that by the time he got back Blanche would be able to travel. He told me he would go back to bring Blandin and Blanche in."

"Who is with Blandin? Only Blanche?"

"Kelso."

"How long have you known Blandin?"

"A few years. I don't know just how many. I haven't kept track of them."

"Where did you first meet him?"

"In the Klondike."

Randall seemed to be partly satisfied. He shoved the pistol into his belt, straightened his huge body and smiled faintly, as if with secret mirth.

"Well, that's right," he said. "Blandin was in the Klondike. Do you know what he was doing there?"

"I never was able to tell," answered Fallon. "At that time I wasn't interested in him. I was going straight, then."

Randall leered at him. He seemed pleased. He laughed loudly and discordantly.

"You found it didn't pay to be good!" he roared. "Well, damme, it don't! The sanctified hypocrites never prosper. Give me a bold and clever thief or an impudent gentleman of the highway, or a freebooter with a lust for blood and a fondness for the ladies, and I'll show you a man!"

He now squinted his eye critically at Fallon and it gleamed with admiration.

"You're a bold, impudent lad yourself," he said. "You've got courage or you wouldn't have looked me straight in the eye when I opened the door upon you. For you'd been told by Blandin what sort of a man I am. Did he tell you?"

Although Fallon had no feeling except that of contempt for the vulgar braggart, he smiled a straight-lipped smile and met Randall's gaze fairly.

"If I hadn't heard of you I would know from looking at the flag yonder."

RANDALL laughed. "So you noticed my coat of arms, eh?" he said. "Well, there's no secret about it. That baby Jolly Roger was made by a fair hand, lad; and if it wasn't for a few jelly-spined lubbers, its mate would still be flying at the masthead of a ship that was once a terror of the seas! Men and fortunes change— damn them!"

Randall's solitary eye gleamed ferociously, and for an instant he stood rigid as if daring Fallon to disagree with him. But Fallon, playing the part he had chosen, maintained a sober and respectful mien.

"It's a way they have," he answered carelessly. He looked straight at Randall, adding:

"I've been traveling north since dawn. I'm in a better mood for food and sleep than for talk. A word from you and I receive the hospitality of your house—or I travel south again to-night."

Randall smiled crookedly, but his eye gleamed.

"Spoken like a man!" he said. "Damn me, I'll take a chance on you. It's been years since I've met a man with courage enough to be impertinent to me. The sort of slobs that I usually have around me are like Goodhull, here, and Revella, who are boot-lickers until they get drunk. Then they are only half men, but imagine themselves fighters. Ain't that so?"

He swung around and faced the men who had sat with him in the chairs outside. During Fallon's presence in the room they had said nothing; and they said nothing now. Revella's skin flushed darkly, and his black eyes flashed with murderous hate over the insult, though his gaze went immediately to the table top. The other man—Goodhull—gave no indication that he had heard.

"Avast!" Randall shouted. "Clear out of here and let me talk to a man!"

Both men rose as a unit. Goodhull moved quickly after he got to his feet, but Revella paused at the table edge, deliber-ately turned and faced Fallon, straightened his necktie, brushed some imaginary dust from the sleeves of his coat and smiled suavely.

"So M'sieur Fallon has the courage to be impertinent? It is marvelous! Pleasant dreams, M'sieur Fallon."

His black eyes, flaming with hate, met Fallon's. Fallon had not exchanged words with the man, but he realized that as sometimes happens between men, there had been aroused in Revella an instinctive hostility and antagonism, which had been aggravated by Lumly Randall's insult.

As Fallon watched Revella stride out of the room there was something about the man that made him think of a hidden knife, of stealthy attacks in the dark, of poison or a noose. And once again he became aware of the peculiar odor of the room—of the blood odor that the renovating power of fresh water and paint could not remove.

CHAPTER XV

A LAUGHING JUDAS

THERE WAS ONE thing about Lumly Randall's manner that at first had rather eluded Fallon. He had not been able to determine exactly what it was until Randall had ridiculed and insulted Goodhull and Revella. It was the man's insincerity.

In his voice, in his manner, in the gleaming of his solitary eye was a sardonic and hideous insincerity, a ribald inward and hidden passion for double dealing. The man would pretend friendliness and all the time he would be plotting destruction. It was duplicity of the sort that would permit him to smile with engaging joviality at a man who at his orders was being forced to walk the plank. It was the insincerity of the man who reaches out a hand to lead you into the pit.

And now, having plumbed Lumly Randall's character, Fallon knew that Randall was plotting his destruction. He knew that Randall had not believed his story that he was a friend of Blandin's. He had pretended that he was being convinced, but he was too wily a rogue to accept, unsupported, any man's word.

It might be that he half believed Fallon, and had granted him the hospitality of the stone house until he could really convince himself that his guest was speaking the truth; but now as Fallon faced him after the disappearance of Goodhull and Revella, he was aware of the Gargantuan mirth lurking behind the eye that stared at him.

He told Fallon to kick his pack into a corner and invited him to stand his rifle near it. He looked at the heavy Colt in the leather sheath at Fallon's side, and his lips curved into a smile.

"A good gun, my lad," he said. "Aye, and I have no doubt you know how to use it. What caliber is it?"

"Forty-five."

"Hefty, I'll warrant. Let me feel its weight."

He held out a hand. But Fallon made no motion to grant the request.

"Its weight is forty ounces, loaded," he answered.

Randall did not appear to be offended over Fallon's tacit refusal to permit him to handle the gun. Instead, he smiled.

"Is it loaded now?"

Fallon nodded.

"I might say that it is an offense against hospitality to bring a loaded gun into your host's house," Randall said; then added: "But you have come in from a long trail. We will let it pass."

He seated himself in one of the chairs at the far side of the table. He was facing the big fireplace and Fallon, who had moved around the room until he was now standing with his back to the fireplace.

Fallon was facing Randall, but from where he stood he could see a blackly yawning doorway at his left and another at his right, opening into darkened rooms. He was squarely between them.

Fallon merely glanced at the doors out of the corners of his eyes. Yet it seemed to him that Randall had taken note of the fact, and that the solitary eye glinted derisively. But Randall's voice was friendly.

"You will dine presently, Fallon," he said. "But first you will answer a few more questions. You see, it was not understood that Blandin was to send me a guest, and I want to inquire more closely into the circumstances that sent you here. There is no hurry, unless you are very hungry. In the meantime here is some very excellent Burgundy." He pushed bottle and glass toward Fallon.

Fallon walked the distance to the table, a full fifteen feet, and filled a glass with the dark purple wine. While Fallon filled the glass Randall did not move, but sat leaning back in his chair, his hands braced against the edge of the table, watching his guest's face.

The glass filled, Fallon looked at Randall, smiled, stepped back a little so that he could see Randall while he drank, and slowly drained the glass. Then he stepped forward again, set the glass on the table and moved slowly backward until he was again standing close to the big fireplace.

Fallon had been very deliberate in his drinking, yet all the while Randall had not moved. His good eye was as steady as an agate and quite as hard. His nose, which was hooked at the bridge like an eagle's beak, was abnormally prominent in the dim light from the single oil lamp, and the leather patch over his blind eye accentuated the villainous cast of his face.

His lips wore an odd expression; it seemed they were pursed to assist him in the process of thinking, for they moved into various crooked angles and curves as he continued to watch Fallon, revealing the passions that stirred him.

THAT he was mentally debating some sort of evil, Fallon was certain. He had not yet reached a decision, and in attempting to do so he was considering the situation carefully.

There was Fallon's gun to be thought of. Forty ounces, it weighed—loaded. Perhaps he was considering the slight emphasis Fallon had placed on the "loaded." Perhaps he was wondering how quickly Fallon could draw the gun, and how well he could shoot it afterward. He might be wondering how strong Fallon was, how quickly he could move.

Something was being pondered in the brain behind his swinish face, beneath the low, receding forehead—urge and doubt, lust and cunning and caution were weighing the possibility of failure.

At last the hideous lips curved into a smirk, and once again Fallon got the feeling that great and hideous mirth had gripped the man. But Fallon was never more cool than now, never more alert and prepared.

"Damn me, you're a man, Fallon!" said Randall. He took his hands from the table edge and folded them over his great chest. Above the edge of the table Fallon could see the butt of the pistol in his belt. The right hand was poised directly above it. A single movement would draw it, if that was Randall's intention.

"You're a man, Fallon!" he repeated. And once more Fallon could detect reluctant admiration in his eye. "You are as strong as a bull moose. I'll warrant those muscles of yours could twist a man's head off. All day you've been on a hard trail—none harder—and yet you stand there, balancing yourself on your toes like a runner. I'd liked to have had you with me in the old days...

"That's a replica of the ship I sailed, Fallon. A beauty, eh? She could outsail anything on the seven seas. Aye, and outrun them, too, when it happened she had to. Look at the lines of her, man. Did you ever see anything like her?"

Fallon turned his head for the split part of a second; turned it back again as quickly, and slipped his lithe body sidewise as he caught the glint of the long-bladed knife that had already left Lumly Randall's right hand and was flashing toward him like a streak of light, straight for his throat.

As Fallon moved sidewise, he was also moving forward. In two leaps he had covered the space between the mantel and Randall, and as he heard the knife ring against the stone breast of the fireplace his heavy Colt was in his right hand. He saw Randall clawing at the pistol in his belt. In the pirate's astonishment over the failure of the knife to find its target and his eagerness to kill, his hand had faltered.

Before he could draw the pistol Fallon's body, coming feet first over the table, was upon him. Fallon's feet struck his chest, and Randall crashed backward, the chair under him. The back of his head struck the stone floor with a sound like that which would be made by a coconut shell cracking. His face turned instantly ashen and his huge body grew limp.

Standing over him, gun in hand, Fallon looked down at him. A thin trickle of red appeared under Randall's head and spread slowly over the surface of the stone upon which he rested. The impact of Fallon's body striking Randall had been terrific, but there had been little sound. The ring of the knife against the stone chimney, the sudden crack of Randall's skull cracking on the stone floor, the crash of the wooden chair, muffled by Randall's weight, had been all.

Fallon stood erect and sheathed his gun. His gaze roved around the room. It went to the two doors—one east, one west; to the fireplace. He saw the knife. It was a heavy weapon, weighing, he judged, three or four pounds. The blade was fifteen or sixteen inches long, the haft was short. A good knife to throw, and Randall had thrown it well. The knife had not fallen to the floor. It was lying on the mantel, its razor-like edge gleaming in the light from the bracket lamp.

Randall was unconscious, and would probably die. At any rate there was little probability of his recovering consciousness for some time. So, leaving him where he had fallen, Fallon walked to the front wall and took down the bracket lamp. He lowered the wick a little so that the blaze would not smudge the lamp chimney when he walked, then returned to the mantel and picked up the knife Randall had thrown.

A terrible weapon. Had he been unsuspicious—had he even been a fractional part of a second later in turning the knife, flung with terrific force, would have been buried to the haft in his throat.

HE LOOKED from the knife to Randall. Randall's huge body was motionless; he had not moved after the fall. His big chin, now more than ever like a bulldog's, was thrust straight upward toward the ceiling. Fallon was in no hurry to help him. He had now an opportunity to explore the house in an effort to find Lin Underhill, and he meant to do it. That was why he had taken the lamp from the bracket.

He gazed into the doorway that opened upon the darkened room eastward. It was the door through which Revella and Goodhull had passed. He would enter that door later. He turned to the west door and abruptly halted, his muscles rigid, while he stared at a vision of loveliness that he was never to forget.

Deep in the darkness beyond the west door, so far away that it seemed to be hundreds of feet distant, appeared the head and shoulders of a woman. She was holding a small lamp in one hand, so that the blaze was just above her head, and the light shone down upon her, framing her head and shoulders in its subdued radiance. Her hair, black and lustrous, was in a filmy cascade as if she had been interrupted while combing it. Through it appeared the perfect oval of her face, the skin like white marble, and her full, firm throat sweeping down in ravishingly graceful curves to a white bosom where a light night garment was caught tightly in her left hand. She was leaning a little forward, listening and watching, and her eyes, wide with fright in their frame of long, velvety lashes, were gazing at him with a strange mixture of fear and astonishment and wonder.

Fallon drew a breath so deep that he feared his lungs would burst. Some unsuspected emotion was tugging at him, a latent force which he never before had experienced, was stirring him. The blood in his body seemed to drain until his cheeks were chalk white. Then it returned, surging and leaping in his veins like fire, filling him with a strange ecstasy, awakening in him a desire that he had never known.

He must have been a fearsome figure to the woman as he stood in front of the fireplace, the oil lamp in his left hand, its light shining upon him, the long-bladed knife in his right hand. He must have been a vision to conjure thoughts of murder in the woman's mind.

She must have heard Randall's chair overturn, or perhaps she had heard the knife ring against the stone wall of the chimney breast. Something had brought her with the light to investigate, and now fright was holding her in the spot where she had stood when she had caught sight of Fallon. For now, watching her, Fallon observed that she drew her breath with a gasp, and that the lamp swayed in her hand as if about to fall.

For an instant the chimney toppled. But presently it steadied. The woman stood motionless for a time, intently watching Fallon. And then, after a little while, seeming to overcome her fright, she straightened proudly and began to walk forward, toward him.

CHAPTER XVI

NIGHT PROWLING

FALLON PLACED THE bracket lamp upon the mantel shelf and laid the knife beside it—by way of assuring her that whatever had happened previous to her appearance, she herself was to be immune to harm. His real purpose was to encourage her to come nearer so that he might speak to her. For a time, watching her in the far-off darkness, he had entertained a fear that she might not be real.

She was real enough, though. He was convinced of that when at last she stood in the open doorway within twenty or thirty feet of him, looking at him.

The marble-white pallor of her face was now tinged with color, as a blush ran quickly up her throat and spread over her face, adding a vital radiance to her appearance. Her eyelashes drooped, and there was a queer, defiant shyness in her eyes, which were very clear and very determined. It was plain that she intended to discover what had happened, and that no consideration of modesty or embarrassment would deter her.

For the first time in his life Fallon was embarrassed before a woman. Mrs. Hammond had told him that when he wanted a woman he would take her. He had always known that. He had never yet wanted one, until now. And now that she was standing before him, he knew that he could not and would not take her after the manner he had always confidently expected he would—with a ruthlessness and impetuosity that would sweep her off her feet and into his arms.

No. A swift and startling change had come over him. Respect, reverence, gentleness were the emotions that now gripped him. His steady eyes had a softness in them, a flame that betrayed him. He could feel his cheeks burning; he was aware that his breath was coming fast, and yet he had no power to control it.

He said nothing. The woman continued to watch him. Her gaze roved over him from head to foot, quickly, and returned immediately to his face, which she studied searchingly as if in an effort to determine what sort of a man he was, if she had anything to fear from him, whether she should cry out for help—or endeavor to deal with him herself.

It appeared she decided to follow the latter course; and perhaps she observed Fallon's embarrassment, and was influenced by it, for the wonderful eyes grew slightly amused and her lips curved into a faint smile.

"What are you doing here?" she asked.

Fallon had known that her voice would be like that—low, carefully modulated, calm. It matched her dark beauty. Her fright had vanished, and she was now confident and serene. She appeared to be unconscious of the garment she wore—or rather she wore it as she might have worn more pretentious apparel, with the simple dignity and grace that identifies those who are accustomed to such things.

"I am a guest."

Fallon observed her eyes grow cold. They seemed to gleam with a slight contempt.

"Your pardon, *m'sieur.* I did not mean to intrude upon the amusements of one of Lumly Randall's guests. Nor did I deliberately attempt to spy upon your somewhat amazing actions. I thought I heard an odd noise, and I came to investigate. Do you always roam around at night carrying a lamp and a knife, *m'sieur?*"

The mockery in her voice steadied Fallon. At a stroke it sobered him.

He smiled and bowed, adding:

"I have some bad habits, ma'am. One of them is that whenever a knife is thrown at me I invariably dodge."

"A commendable action, I believe." She seemed not to take him seriously, for her smile was mocking, though she was certainly admiring his muscular body, his bold eyes and his handsome face. And she was thoughtfully considering his words, trying to understand his meaning, for plainly she had not yet observed Lumly Randall lying on the floor with the overturned chair under him and his blood creeping over the stone.

SHE LOOKED at the knife on the mantel shelf.

"Is that Lumly Randall's knife?" she asked. "Did he throw it at you?"

Fallon nodded.

Her eyes widened; apprehension filled them.

"Where is Lumly Randall?" she whispered.

Fallon pointed, watching her.

She gasped, drew her nightrobe tighter. Her cheeks blanched. For an instant she closed her eyes, swayed; then, hesitatingly, she moved to where Randall was lying, and stood, with both hands pressed to her bosom, gazing down at him.

She shivered when she observed the blood on the slab of stone under Randall's head.

"Dead?" she whispered. "Did you kill him?"

"He fell," said Fallon. "He is not dead. He may not die."

"He must not die!" she declared passionately.

She stood erect, facing Fallon. Some strong passion gripped her. It was not regret, or grief.

Fallon decided that Randall was not even a relative, and that her eagerness to have the man live was based upon some obscure reason that she would keep to herself.

"There is no doctor here, of course?" said Fallon.

"Yes. Meeson. He is an old man. He belonged to Lumly Randall's old crew—to his ship, the Terror. I hate him! And yet we must keep Lumly Randall from dying if possible. We *must!*"

"We'll do what we can. Is Meeson in this house?"

"Yes. He has a room in the west wing, under the tower. Will you go for him, while I summon Revella and Goodhull and the others to carry Randall to his room? Take a lamp and go through that door."

She pointed to the room from which she had entered.

"At the far end of the room you will find a hallway," she continued. "To your right. At its end, go up the stairs, and down that hall to the end door. Knock upon it four times—twice softly and twice loudly. Meeson will answer, if he isn't too drunk. Tell him what has happened. Tell him I want him to come immediately. Hurry, please!"

Fallon looked back as he reached the west door. The woman was hastening toward the east door, and had drawn her night-robe tightly to her, so that it would not impede her progress. He saw her white heels twinkling in the dim lamplight above the sandals she wore.

Fallon did not share her eagerness. Randall was nothing to him, and the man had tried to kill him. He would feel no grief over Randall's death. He was more interested in what he might find on the second floor of the house—in the tower itself, if perchance he could find an entrance to it.

Also, he would be interested in the rooms he passed, for one of them might conceal the man he was seeking, Lin Underhill.

He took his time going through the next room. It was obviously a lounging room, for there were big chairs here and there, two great lounges, some bear skins on the stone slabs that formed the floor, and several heavy card tables with gambling paraphernalia.

Fallon was little interested in the furnishings. There were four large windows equipped with glass and heavy wooden bars, but the shutters had not yet been closed, and Fallon moved to one of the windows and stood before it for an instant, holding the light so that its beams shone fairly upon him.

He knew that Wattanooka would be watching, and this was

one of the signals that had been agreed upon before Fallon entered the house. The signal he had given, as agreed, indicated to the old Indian that Fallon was having no trouble.

Leaving the window, he made his way through the room, and strode down the hall, inspecting several doors he passed and carefully trying their fastenings. All were closed, locked. At each door he listened, but there came no sound to indicate that any one inside the rooms had heard him try the doors.

HE REACHED the stairs, slowly climbed them, and found himself in the upper hall. The woman had told him that at the end of the hallway he would find a door, but he found there were half a dozen doors opening from the hallway, and that as he had entered the hall about midway, there were two ends, and a door at each.

He tried the east door first, and there was no response to his knock. As he stood before the door, listening, he heard sounds that seemed to come from a distance; a noise as of boots on a wooden floor, footsteps on stairs; voices raised in alarm. He heard them only faintly and was convinced that they came through the wall at the end of the hall. If that were the case, then the stone wall at the end of the hall must divide the house, and there must be rooms on the other side.

Revella and Goodhull had gone into the room to the east, downstairs, and in order to reach their sleeping quarters they would have to use a stairway. And so far as Fallon could see, the stairway he had used was the only one, unless, as he suspected, there were two sections to the house, divided by the stone wall, and each section having its own stairway.

He went to the other end of the hallway, trying all the doors as he passed them. There was no response to his knocking, and he finally reached the last door. He decided that this was the northwest corner of the house and that one of the towers was directly above the room before whose door he stood. There was no stairway leading upward. There might be one outside the house, but that was improbable.

He knocked on the door. There was no answer. He knocked again, and this time a gruff voice replied:

"Who's there?"

"Are you Meeson?" asked Fallon.

"Yes, damn you, whoever you are! Let a man sleep, can't you?"

"You're wanted in the big room downstairs," Fallon informed him. "Randall's been hurt. Skull's crushed."

"It's time the big slob got it crushed," growled Meeson. "I've been on the point of crushing it myself a dozen times. All right; I'll be down. Who's that—Killen? Mortwell? Atkins? Eccles?"

Fallon did not answer. He retreated to the east end of the hall and flattened himself in one of the doorways, behind the wide, heavy jambs. He blew out the lamp, first making certain he had matches with which to light it again, and stood, waiting, for he had resolved to enter Meeson's room if possible, hoping it would lead him into the tower.

Meeson was taking his time. Apparently he liked Lumly Randall but little, if at all.

There were now no sounds from the lower floor. There was no sound from Meeson's room. The atmosphere in the hallway was heavy and musty, as if no air from the outside had ever reached it. The stone floor of the hall was damp, the walls were clammy with moisture. The silence was tomb-like.

But presently Fallon heard a door creak on its hinges and a beam of light appeared on the wall opposite Meeson's door. Meeson's shadow—a short, fat man.

He came out into the hall, carrying a lamp. He locked the door and pocketed the huge key. The light from the lamp shone on his face as he walked down the hall toward the stairs. Meeson had a heavy, dissolute face. His hair was gray, sparse, tousled. He was grinning, talking to himself. "The old skull-cracker finally got his own cracked, eh? Heh, heh, heh!"

He went down the stairs, the light dancing after him; and Fallon moved down the hall toward the room he had just vacated.

CHAPTER XVII

THE MAN WITH THE RAPIER

EVEN FALLON'S GREAT strength was not sufficient to break the massive lock of Meeson's door, so after a while he ceased his efforts and stood in the hallway, panting from his determined attacks.

The hallway was dark, for Fallon had not relighted his lamp, and there were no windows to let in light from the outside. Temporarily baffled, Fallon waited in the darkness, thinking of his adventures of the night.

He had accomplished something already. In cracking Randall's skull he had disposed of the one man who might have denied him the privilege of staying in the house. Randall had not believed his story, of course, or he would not have thrown the knife.

Even if Randall lived it would be many days before he would be able to remember what had happened to him, and by that time Fallon hoped to find Underhill. In the meantime the other members of the household would be forced to consider him Randall's guest, for both Revella and Goodhull had been in the big room downstairs when Randall had accepted him.

But now, although he was as eager as ever to fulfill his mission, he was aware of an added interest in life. There had been other girls who had arrested his attention. But not for long. Not one had been of the type of which he had dreamed—the steady, serious, serene and mature woman who would take her place by his side, prepared to meet what might come. He had been patient, knowing that there were such women in the world. And now he had met one.

Like all the great adventures of life, this one had burst upon him unexpectedly. In this sinister house in the center of a vast wilderness, among thieves and cutthroats, she had appeared to him in the darkness. Her beauty had not been marred; her sturdy, uncompromising honesty shone out of her wonderful eyes. He did not know how she happened to be living in the stone house, surrounded by men like Lumly Randall and the others. Nor did he care.

He relighted the lamp and strode down the hall, retracing his steps to the big room. He had not succeeded in getting into Meeson's room, but he intended to have another try before the night was over.

When he reached the big room there was no one in it but the woman, and she was sitting in a big chair before the fireplace. She did not seem to be aware of Fallon's presence, for she sat gazing straight before her, at the miniature ship on the mantel shelf; but she asked:

"What is your name, *monsieur?*"

"Jim Fallon."

"Jim Fallon," she repeated. "That is an Irish name, is it not? Mine is Denise Laville. It is French—so I am told. There—we are acquainted. And I do not fear you as much as when I first saw you—with the knife in your hand." She nodded her head toward the east door of the room. "Meeson and the others have taken him to his room," she added. "He is hurt very badly."

SHE TURNED in the chair and looked at Fallon. She was now facing the lamp, and Fallon saw that her eyes were a chestnut brown. They were narrowed with interest.

"You are Lumly Randall's guest, *monsieur?*"

"Yes."

"Why did you come here?"

"Blandin sent me."

Her lips tightened. Her eyes flashed once, then they were serene again.

"Blandin and Lumly Randall are friends," she said. "If Blandin sent you here, why did Lumly Randall try to kill you?"

"I cannot answer that."

"I can," she said. "Blandin did not send you. Randall suspected you of being an impostor, and you are."

Fallon did not answer. Yet her frankness amazed him, brought a slow smile to his lips. Denise Laville was a very disconcerting young woman. She was not, he decided, more than twenty-two or three, yet the gravity of her expression, the steady serenity of her gaze were, in his experience, associated with women of a more mature age. He realized there was little hope of successfully lying to her.

"You are an impostor, aren't you?" she persisted.

"If you mean that Blandin did not send me here—yes."

"I knew it."

"I should like to know how you happened to read my thoughts."

"Not your thoughts, *monsieur*. Your face. Wicked men do not blush when alone with women. Ah, I have seen them. And a minute ago, when you told me that Blandin had sent you, I knew you were lying. You see, *monsieur*, I have met many wicked men since I have lived in this house. Only once was there a good man, and he did not stay long. Like you, *monsieur*, he blushed when we were brought together. After he disappeared—very suddenly—I overheard Lumly Randall say of him: 'Too damned good to have around.' Those were Lumly Randall's words."

She was still facing him, studying him. Her eyes were pools of conjecture and interest. There was wistfulness in them also, and the dawning of a fugitive hope.

"Ah, *monsieur*, if I only dared to think so!" she said, her voice almost a whisper.

"If you only dared to think what?"

"That you have come—that you are here to search for Lin Underhill!"

Fallon's muscles stiffened; a pulse of contempt ran over him. His lips tightened. Was this woman a Delilah, sent to tempt him? Were there men concealed in the darkened rooms waiting to pounce upon him if he confessed his real errand?

Yet he smiled at her. Already he had confessed that he had not been sent by Blandin. The spell of her was upon him. Cynically he had watched other men yield to the lure and witchery of a beautiful face, realizing they were merely victims of their passions, sacrificing their manhood for a few hours of pleasure. And he had told himself that never would he be so tempted. But until now he had never known passion—such passion as this woman had inspired.

He had already committed himself. If she had fooled him so far he was trapped, and he would meet his death in this house. He laughed softly, as at a grim jest.

"I came to search for Underhill."

He stepped back so that he could see both the east and west doors, and his right hand hovered over the butt of the heavy revolver at his right hip.

Nothing happened. There were no sounds except those that were being made by the scraping of boots on the stone floors above, and he had heard these sounds ever since he had entered the room. They indicated to him that Lumly Randall's friends were working over him, probably under Meeson's orders.

And now there came another sound. Denise Laville was crying.

Amazed, Fallon stood, watching her.

He was about to move toward her when he heard a slow step on a distant stairway. It seemed to come through the east door. A step, descending.

Fallon observed that Denise had also heard it, for she sprang erect, quickly dried her eyes with a handkerchief, and placed an admonishing finger to her lips. Her moist eyes and that warning finger satisfied him that his suspicions had been unjust. He smiled at her as both stood listening to the descending footsteps, and his heart leaped with a great joy when she returned the smile.

THE STEPS came on. They echoed hollowly in the darkness beyond the east door, and they were accompanied by a metallic clanking as of a sword sheath striking a man's boot. The latter sound was new, and Fallon concluded that while on the stairs the sheath had been lifted. Therefore the wearer must now be on the level floor of the room eastward and the sheath was dangling from its straps.

Out of Denise's smile came the words:

"Denatti—the exquisite."

The gay mockery in her voice was contradicted by the pallor which swept over her face. She feared Denatti, whoever he was.

She crossed the room, and as she passed Fallon she whispered: "Do not tell Denatti what you have told me." She paused at the front door, which was closed, and pretended to peer outward into the night At the instant the newcomer strode into the room from the east door, she was again crossing to the mantel, giving the man the impression that while she was in the room with Fallon she had not been engaged in conversation with him.

Denatti hesitated slightly as he reached the door. He darted quick glances at Fallon and Denise, and around the room. Then he strode forward, to halt within half a dozen paces of Fallon and stare at him impudently.

He was arrayed in knee-length trousers of black velvet, a black velvet coat rakishly cut at the waist, so that it flared slightly outward; a white, ruffled shirt, a broad scarlet sash, a ruffled collar and a flowing tie. The sleeves of his coat were wide and loose at the cuffs, revealing a trace of white linen. He was hatless, and he wore glistening boots with low, soft tops. His finger tips touched the tops of the boots as he bowed to Denise.

He was a handsome rogue. And rogue he was, from his glossy

black hair to the toes of the spotless boots. His skin was a light olive, made lighter by face powder; his eyes were black, flashing, arrogant. They burned with the light of bold desire as they rested on Denise, who held her head high and gave him back a straight, disdainful stare; they flamed with cold hate when they met Fallon's, though Fallon's gaze was expressionless.

A fop, a dandy, was Denatti. A swashbuckling imitation gentleman of a past age—the mate of a privateer—a gallant with the ladies of a Latin court? Denatti could be any of these, but it was highly probable that he was a son of a decadent line, because, in spite of his well-cut features, there was in his face evidence of a brutal and dissolute nature which had not been acquired, but had been bequeathed him.

His gaze returned to Denise; he ignored Fallon.

"Mlle. Denise is ravishing to-night," he said, his voice low and soft and filled with a boldness which told her that he had taken note of the night garment she wore.

Denise's head went a little higher.

"M. Denatti is always the insincere flatterer," she answered. Her disdain of Denatti was so apparent that it brought a twitching smile to Fallon's lips.

"It is discouraging," said Denatti. "But if Mlle. Denise will not accept my admiration perhaps she will be good enough to present her friend." He stood, his left hand on his sword hilt, insolently staring at Fallon.

Was it jealousy that now assailed Fallon and sent fire instead of blood surging through his veins? Had it been Denatti's glance at Denise's night garment that roused in him the murderous rage that flamed in his eyes?

Slowly, deliberately, he turned his back to Denatti and walked to the front door, where he stood, shading his eyes with his hands to gaze out.

This house! It was peopled with cutthroats who masqueraded in grotesque and preposterous raiment. They were ghosts of yesterday treading to-day's stage, making their appearance from various dark corners, clanging down stairways with swords dangling at their sides.

Cockney sailors posing as halberdiers; a fat doctor croaking about broken skulls; a pirate ship on the mantel bearing the black flag with its skull and crossbones; Revella, a foppish devil posing as a gentleman; Lumly Randall with his owlish secrecy and his loud boasts of conquests; the room with its odor of blood. Denatti and his insolent staring.

Denatti crossed the room behind Fallon, his right hand gripping the hilt of his sword. He stood behind Fallon and gently tapped Fallon's shoulder.

"Insolent lout!" he said. "Stand clear that I may spit you!"

CHAPTER XVIII

IN THE HOUSE OF MYSTERY

DENATTI'S SWORD WAS half drawn when Fallon's hands closed over it. A prodigious wrench and the sword snapped off at the hilt. The blade clanked back into the scabbard, and the handle, equipped with a silver basket guard, clattered to the floor.

One of Fallon's hands went out and gripped Denatti's throat. A squeeze, and Denatti's head rolled. A vigorous shove, and Denatti reeled, staggered backward, and brought up against one of the stone columns, his mouth open, gasping for breath.

And then, as Fallon moved after him, wary, his muscles alive with eagerness, his lips tight, and his eyes a light with the sudden passion that Denatti had aroused, Denatti sought to draw a pistol from his waist, beneath the sash.

It was then that Denise heard, the first time in her life, the sodden thud of a fist striking flesh. She saw the blow struck, heard it land, and watched Denatti strike the floor, face down, to lie there, unconscious.

And then, in a frenzy of fear, she was pulling at Fallon's arm, trying to drag him out of the room.

"Is he dead?" she asked.

"No. He'll be a little dizzy for a while, but he'll get over that, too."

"Then come!" she whispered. "Let us get out of here before Denatti recovers. You are a brave, strong man, but you cannot fight all of them. Come, please?"

Denise went to the table, took up the lamp, and led the way up the stairs that Fallon had climbed in searching for Meeson's room. With Fallon standing close to her, she took a huge key from a case which was suspended from a girdle around her waist, unlocked a door, entered, and motioned Fallon to follow. Then she closed the door, locked it from the inside, and stood there for an instant with the light shining upon her wondrous face, panting and listening.

"Oh!" she said. "I was afraid they were coming!"

But no sound came from below.

There were three windows in this room, which, Fallon instantly divined, was Denise's. The windows were open, and from the dense timber around the house came the night noises of the denizens of the wild. Also, as Fallon and Denise stood there listening, they heard the faint footsteps of the halberdiers as they strode back and forth on the granite slope outside.

DENISE'S room, unlike the hallways and other rooms that Fallon had seen, was cheerful. He was aware of light, delicate curtains, of decorations and ornaments that were distinctly feminine; of a bed with a gay counterpane and pillow slips, of tassels and pictures and plaques and statuettes; of laces and ribbons and silken garments. But he was aware of them only as a setting for the woman who now stood before him, shrinking a little from him, trembling a little, trying to smile at him, trying to convey to him the message that she had brought him here merely to provide sanctuary.

She waved him to a chair, and sat in one near him, breathlessly watching him, wondering, perhaps, if she had acted wisely in bringing him to her room.

"It is the first time, *monsieur*," she said, blushing.

"The first time for what?"

"The first time there has been—" She hesitated, confused, and finished resolutely, "The first time a man has ever entered my room."

"Let's get out of here," she begged. "You can't fight all of them!"

"I know it," answered Fallon bluntly. He frowned. "But Denatti would need no second invitation. Most men are wolves."

She smiled serenely. Her color had become normal.

"Men like Denatti aren't so bad," she said, shrugging her shoulders a little. "They rely upon their good looks, thinking that women will fall into their arms. Denatti is a peacock. I am not afraid of men like Denatti. A look, a disdainful glance, will silence him. It is men like Blandin that I fear. I met Blandin twice. The first time he leered at me; the second time he tried to crowd me into a dark hallway."

Fallon clenched his hands. His lips went into straight lines.

"I mean to kill Blandin," he declared.

"I have seen so much of that. I have not actually witnessed it, of course," she added. "But I know it has been done."

Fallon thought of the odor in the big room downstairs.

"How long have you lived here?"

"I am twenty-three. They tell me that I was about three when I was brought here."

"Is Randall any relation to you?"

"No. My father was first mate on Lumly Randall's ship, the Terror, a pirate ship. My mother was on a ship that was captured by the Terror. They murdered all the men of the captured ship, and they drew lots for my mother. My father won her. She was not molested by any of the other men. Lumly Randall and my father were great friends. I do not know what happened to the Terror. My first recollection of anything is that Lumly Randall, my mother and some other men were in an open boat, at sea. Afterward everything is vague. There was a city, fine clothes, luxuries. And I have a mental picture of my mother. And yet the picture is mostly great, sad, dark eyes and a pallor. I think my mother grieved greatly for my father.

"There was never another man. I do not know what happened, but one day mother and I and Lumly Randall were in this house. I have been here ever since. My mother died. She is buried near here.

"Lumly Randall always treated me as a lady. He told me I was a lady, and that some day he would tell me the story and what my mother's name was, before it was changed to Laville. Lumly Randall is a beast and a murderer, but he treated me well."

She paused, listened.

Fallon could hear some one walking in the hallway. The steps paused at the door and a hand shook the fastenings.

"Mademoiselle Laville!" came a voice.

"Yes?"

"Open the door!"

Revella's voice!

"I am undressing, *monsieur!*"

She blushed as she lied, but glanced at Fallon and gave her head a little toss of defiance. She was natural, Fallon decided. In her was no pretense of ignorance in men's desires. Her protection during her stay at the stone house had not been the stupidity of innocence, nor the assumed hard sophistication of experience. She knew men and women, but chose to ignore what was base in them.

REVELLA laughed. "Then Fallon is not in there with you?"

"*Monsieur!*"

She would have made a good actress. There was good counterfeit of indignation in her voice. She was brave, clever, wise, Fallon saw.

Revella laughed again. "Well, you saw him smash Denatti's face in, didn't you? Denatti says you were there."

"Yes. I was there. Denatti drew his sword. Monsieur Fallon only defended himself. But I ran, Revella. I was afraid of Monsieur Fallon."

"You were very discreet, *mademoiselle*. The man is a terrible fighter. He almost killed Randall. Meeson found prints of Fallon's moccasins on Randall's chest. He doubts that Randall will live. If Fallon is in the house we shall kill him. Be on your guard. Pleasant dreams."

They heard Revella's footsteps go down the hall and the stairs. And when there was silence again, Denise whispered, and looked at Fallon with eyes that had suddenly become severe and accusing.

"*Monsieur*, you have lied to me," she said. "You told me Lumly Randall had fallen."

"He threw the knife. I leaped across the table at him and landed with my feet against his chest."

She shook her head and her color receded a little.

"And in doing that you spoiled all chance of ever finding Lin Underhill," she said. "For Randall alone knows where Underhill is hidden. And perhaps he will never be able to tell."

"Was Underhill in the house?"

"He was. For many months he was a prisoner in the east tower. But only a few weeks ago I overheard Randall telling Denatti that he had taken him away from there and that he was now hidden in a place that no one could find. A secret place, it must have been, for Randall and Denatti almost quarreled about it. Denatti told Randall he had as much right to know as Randall himself. But Randall did not tell. He said he meant to get the truth out of Underhill if he had to kill him by inches."

"The truth about what?"

"About the gold mine. Don't pretend, Fallon; you are not a very good dissembler. You know about the mine."

"Yes."

"You are interested in the mine, also?"

"I am interested in finding Lin Underhill for his father and for a girl who loves him."

"Ah! Tell me about her, Fallon! It must be wonderful to be loved!"

"Have you been loved?" Fallon's lips tightened.

"No, *monsieur*. The only men I have seen have been the men that have come to this house. They have been thieves and gamblers and murderers. One man I might have loved had I been able to see more of him. The good man I spoke about. He was much like you."

"You loved him?"

"I might have loved him. I do not know. I did not talk with him. He may have been jealous—and I should not love a jealous man. If he had been brave and faithful, and straightforward, and would trust me completely, I might have loved him. Also, before I should love him I should want to be certain that he had never loved another woman."

Fallon stared at the floor. At one point he did not fit into her specifications—he was undeniably jealous.

He looked up at her.

"You would not love a jealous man, and yet you would not love a man who had been loved by another woman. Isn't that jealousy?"

"I think not. Yet whether it is or not I should not want a man with half a heart." She tapped a foot on the floor and watched it as she added: "I shall not fall in love at first sight. I shall take my time. I shall want to study him. I should want to test him by having him watch another man try to make love to me. Of course I really would not permit that, but I should like to see what he would do."

"A man who would be worthy of loving you would kill him," Fallon declared.

"Would you kill a man who attempted to win from you the woman you loved?"

"I would," said Fallon, frowning at the floor.

"Then you are jealous," she charged. "Why, it was jealousy that caused you to break Denatti's sword and, afterward, to knock him down."

Fallon nodded.

"You did not like the way he spoke about—about my night garment? And yet Denatti really said nothing offensive."

"It was the way he looked at you."

SHE STOOD up and smiled down at him. But Fallon did not look up at her. He sat, staring at the floor, and she gazed lingeringly at his shapely head, with its black hair, which was ruffled and tousled; at his broad shoulders and his mighty arms. A blush burned in her cheeks and her eyes took on a soft radiance. She moved to a small dressing-table and gazed at her reflection in a mirror. Her expression was a blend of curiosity, amazement, and joy. But she was a picture of serenity and coolness when she stepped away from the mirror and again looked at Fallon, who had not moved.

"Monsieur, how do you expect to find Lin Underhill?"

"I am going to stay here until I do. I am going to search the house."

"Mowaki, the Japanese cook, brings food to my rooms, often. There is a roasted fowl in the next room, now. Also there is a bed. That is the room my mother occupied while she stayed here. It has never been touched or disturbed in any manner except by myself, and the connecting door locks from this room. There is an outside door, leading into the hallway, which fastens on the inside. I think you will have to take the room, Fallon, if you expect to stay here to search for Underhill. And you will have to be very careful, for if they see you they will kill you."

A few minutes later, with a lamp in hand, Fallon entered the adjoining room. He closed the door and heard Denise slip the fastenings into place.

The room was about the size of the one he had just left, but its furnishings were severely plain and meager. There were in the room such articles as might have been considered luxurious twenty or twenty-five years before, but time and disuse had exacted their toll. It was, though, a room to satisfy Fallon, who would have been satisfied with the bed alone.

The window shades were down, and the first thing that Fallon did after closing the door was to walk to one of the two windows, push the shade aside and stand there with the lamp in hand. There was a risk in this action, but Fallon ignored it; he must inform Wattanooka that all was well with him.

Dropping the shade, he feasted upon the food that he found on a small table that stood against the wall that divided the room from Denise's. The food was covered with a cloth.

Denise's news that Randall had hidden Underhill in a place known only to Randall himself was disconcerting, for that meant, probably Underhill would not be found in any of the rooms. Yet the rooms must be searched on the chance that Randall had been lying, or had changed his mind.

The search could not be made until later, until he was reasonably certain Randall's friends were asleep; so he took off his moccasins, unstrapped his cartridge belt and pistol, and stretched out on the bed.

He had left the lamp burning, and had gone to sleep lying on his right side, facing a fireplace in the wall that formed one side of the hallway. The fireplace was not as large as the one in front of which he had been standing when Randall had thrown the knife at him, but like the other it was built entirely of stone, with a mantel shelf similar in design and shape.

There was no fire in the grate, and apparently there had been none in it for a long time. Nor were there any ashes on the stone hearth. Apparently the fireplace had not been in use since Denise's mother had died, for as Fallon had gazed at it just before going to sleep he had observed on the hearthstone a thick accumulation of dust.

And now, after having slept for what seemed to him to have been only a few minutes—although in reality he had slept several hours—he opened his eyes suddenly, as a man of the open sometimes awakens when hearing a sharp, strange sound. His faculties were alert, but he did not move. His gaze, oddly enough, was upon the stone hearth of the fireplace, where it had been when he had gone to sleep.

He heard a slight, scraping noise, subdued, muffled, apparently coming from a distance. He listened intently, thinking the sound came from downstairs, or at least from the farther end of the hallway. And while he watched and listened he observed that the hearthstone was in motion. Slowly, little by little, it was being raised by some unseen force beneath it.

CHAPTER XIX

THE LABYRINTH OF TUNNELS

THE LAMP, WHICH was still where Fallon had placed it on the table, was burning, and the room was flooded with its weak, ruddy glare. The lower sashes of the two windows in the room were open, and a slight, chill breeze came in, bearing with it the dank, moist, spruce-laden scent of the forest and the diapason of the night insects. There was no sound from inside the house except the dull, heavy rasping of the hearthstone as it was stealthily raised.

Fallon made no sound as he sat erect and twisted himself around on the edge of the bed so that he faced the fireplace. His revolver was lying on the bed where he had placed it. He slipped his moccasins on his feet, buckled the cartridge belt about his waist, drew out the heavy revolver and twirled the cylinder to make certain it was filled, then cautiously crossed the room and stepped behind the west end of the chimney breast.

The breast was deep, and by flattening himself against the wall he could conceal himself from the intruder. He did not extinguish the light, for it might have been seen already, and putting it out would warn the uninvited visitor that his presence under the hearthstone had been discovered. And Fallon was very curious.

Peering around the corner of the chimney, Fallon watched the hearthstone. It moved only slightly, with a twisting, heaving motion, as though whoever was under it was exerting his lifting force in its center. It was fitted loosely in its stone frame, and Fallon could see no reason why a great deal of force should be required to move it.

The explanation came presently, however, when at each side of the stone finally appeared the links of an iron chain, the links so fashioned as to form handles by which the stone might be lifted from above. And now Fallon observed that in the stone frame were two loose stones, one on each side, which hid the chain handles from view. Whoever wished to lift the hearthstone from above needed only to remove the stones covering the handles.

But what was under the hearthstone? Fallon speculated upon this question as he watched the stone slowly rise. Gail Hammond had told him that this was a very mysterious house, with towers and secret rooms, and subterranean passages and channels in it, but it seemed that in addition to these there were secret passages from room to room. It must be that in the thick walls and under or between the heavy floors there was room for a system of secret passages which would permit the unscrupulous inmates of the house to murder people in their beds.

Fallon now had no doubt that Revella or some of the others had discovered that he had been in Denise Laville's room, and suspected she had hidden him in the room that had belonged to her mother. Being aware of the secret passages, they were now coming to kill him.

The stone came clear of its socket. It was lifted only a few inches above the level of the stone frame around it, and then it began to move backward, toward the arch of the fireplace. Two great, brown hands were moving it, and a mass of black hair appeared in the vaultlike opening. Then a head and a pair of brawny brown shoulders emerged, and for an instant were motionless as their owner stared at the bed.

The head turned, and two black, penetrating eyes rested upon Fallon. A wide mouth curved and stretched into a delighted grin.

"Ugh!" whispered the intruder. "Wattanooka find um!"

SILENTLY Fallon stepped away from the chimney and took his friend's hand. Then, their voices so low that they could not be heard even by Denise in the next room, they spoke of the secret passage which opened in the fireplace.

Wattanooka was covered with cobwebs, which he brushed from his coppery body as he talked.

He had watched for Fallon's signals, as he had agreed to do. Then, after dark, he had stolen close to the Indian village and had concealed himself for a time in some brush which was near enough to their camp fire to permit him to overhear what was being said. The Indians were Crees, and he a Chippewa, and he hated them for killing his brother; but he had listened.

The Indians had spoken of a large number of white men who were coming to the stone house. The newcomers were to be used to exterminate the inhabitants of Mercie Valley—the valley which had been for many years in possession of Adam Hammond and his family and the Chippewas who lived there with him. The men who were coming were sea rogues who had been assembled by a man who knew where to find such men. They were accomplished blood-letters.

When Wattanooka had heard all this he had worked his way back to the river to a point where he could watch the house. On his previous trip to the house he had observed some peculiar formations of rocks here and there along the river bank, but he had not got close enough to them to examine them. But this time he inspected them, and had found strange things.

In one formation he had discovered that one of the rocks seemed to have been cut to fit among the others. He found he could move it aside, and when he had done so he was amazed to find an opening to a tunnel. He had gone into the tunnel with a lighted faggot. And he had explored the tunnel for quite a distance, to find that it intersected other tunnels—some large, some small.

He had explored the largest tunnel, and had found chimney-like apertures in the ceiling. These openings had excited his interest, and he had discovered iron ladders running up into them. He had climbed one ladder until he had come to a stone that barred his further progress. Then he had laid his ear to the stone and had heard Fallon's voice, and a woman's.

When Wattanooka reached this point he grinned widely.

"Who woman?" he asked.

"Denise Laville."

"How old?"

"Twenty-three."

"White woman?"

Fallon nodded.

"She child Adam Hammond see here," said Wattanooka. "Hammond tell me girl's mother die. Father die before. Girl stay with Randall. Woman now. Good woman. How she look?"

"She is beautiful."

"Like Gail?"

"Yes."

"It is good. How Randall?"

"Randall had his skull cracked."

"Who crack it—you?"

Fallon nodded, and Wattanooka grinned expansively.

"You strong man. Crack um good?"

"Too good. Randall will die, and he alone knows where Underhill is hidden."

"We find," said Wattanooka. "Come. Look."

Wattanooka whispered to Fallon to go down the shaft under the fireplace, and Fallon was poised over the opening when a slight sound at the door leading to the hallway brought him up rigid. The Indian had heard the sound also, for a finger went to his lips and he, too, became rigid.

THE ROOM was big, and the hall doorway was in a recess at the east of the fireplace, so that it was hardly possible that any one in the hall could have overheard Fallon and Wattanooka whispering; but the two waited to determine what the noise beyond the door might mean.

It was not long before they knew they had not been overheard, for they heard the door creaking from a steady pressure and they knew that some one was testing the strength of the fastenings. As it was unlikely that any one would try to enter so stealthily after hearing voices in the room, it was evident that whoever was outside the door suspected that Fallon was there, asleep.

There was a chance that the prowler would go away, so Fallon and the Indian remained motionless, listening. But no; he was still there. He had ceased shoving at the door, no doubt realizing that the fastenings were in place or were too strong to be broken by the pressure he was able to exert. For now, through a crack in the door came the blade of a long knife. The gleaming metal was under the wooden bar which served as a fastening, and the purpose of the knife wielder was to lift the bar above the sockets. That task accomplished, he had only to swing the door open and enter.

There was a chance that he would succeed, and Wattanooka grinned broadly and touched the blade of his belt-ax.

This was a huge weapon. It had a light, narrow head and a broad, convex blade which had been ground to razorlike sharpness. It resembled a type of Roman battle-ax.

Wattanooka drew it and gripped it by its fluted handle. Then he leaned closer to Fallon and whispered:

"Cree knife." He pointed to the blade which was in the crack of the door. The crack ran at a sharp angle through the heavy wood, so that whoever was outside had not been able to see into the room through it, and it was so small that much time would be required by the knife wielder to enlarge the crack enough to accomplish his purpose.

"You lay on bed—sleep," continued Wattanooka. "Cree open door, see you sleep. Him come in. Wattanooka step on neck."

Fallon obeyed, resting his gun along his thigh, under the

blanket. Wattanooka slipped over into the recess near the door, so that he would be behind it when it opened.

Fallon pretended to sleep. The knife widened the crack under the bar on the door. Grimly Wattanooka watched the whittlings drop to the floor near his feet.

Finally the crack was widened sufficiently to permit the knife to do its work. The bar began to lift, making no noise whatever. It finally went over the top of the socket and was held there. Then the door began to move inward, slowly, an inch at a time.

When halfway open it stopped. The intruder was evidently looking at the supposedly sleeping Fallon.

Apparently he was satisfied. He could see Fallon, and perhaps he could see the edge of the hearthstone and a portion of the hole that gaped at its edge. For as he stepped into the room his head was turned toward the fireplace and his back was toward Wattanooka. The man was an Indian.

And at that instant Wattanooka struck. He had been holding the belt-ax in his left hand, and as he struck, his right hand gripped the Cree's knife-hand. The heavy poll of the ax landed with a queer, hollow thump on the top of the Cree's head; and so swiftly was it done that Fallon, who had opened his eyes at the instant, saw only a faint glint as the metal cleaved the air.

The Cree slumped forward without a sound. He was doubled forward in Wattanooka's arms when Fallon slipped out of the bed, and his long knife had dropped from his loosening fingers into Wattanooka's right hand.

Wattanooka handled the Cree as an ordinary man would handle a child. With his right hand holding the Cree's knife, he closed the door and softly dropped the bar into place. Then, with Fallon watching him curiously, he laid the Cree on the floor, face up, and placed a moccasined foot on his neck. As Fallon started forward to interfere, his black eyes flashed warningly, and he whispered through grim lips:

"No, Fallon. Cree kill my brother, cut um up. Wattanooka

kill Cree—step on neck. 'Leven, now. Cree see foot on neck—know who do."

Fallon comprehended. The foot on the Cree's neck was Wattanooka's trade-mark, his insignia of vengeance. The blow with the ax had already killed the Cree. But Fallon turned his back in distaste.

AFTER a while, when he heard a sound behind him, he turned to see Wattanooka carrying the Cree through the doorway. Wattanooka vanished down the hallway, leaving the door open. When he returned, ax in hand, he grunted the one word, "Good!"

Grinning at Fallon as though nothing had happened, he pointed to the shaft under the hearthstone.

Fallon went down, his moccasined feet feeling for the rungs of the iron ladder which was fastened against a stone wall. After he had descended a little distance he saw Wattanooka enter the shaft. For a time the Indian remained at the top, evidently arranging the chain handles of the hearthstone so that they would not be seen; and then the light in the room was blotted out, and Fallon could hear Wattanooka's feet slithering lightly on the iron rungs as he descended.

The distance down was not great, for the ceilings of the house were low, and presently Fallon felt his feet come in contact with a stone floor. He moved away from the ladder and a moment later he felt Wattanooka beside him. A sulphur match flared up, burning with a greenish-yellow flame and assailing Fallon's nostrils with its acrid odor, and in its light he saw Wattanooka stooping to ignite a faggot which he had evidently left at the foot of the ladder when he had prepared to ascend the shaft.

The men were in a tunnel-like passage which had been cut through rotted rock. It was irregular in shape, but its makers had apparently attempted to follow a circular pattern. The atmosphere, musty with the vitiated air of a quarter of a century, was like that of an ancient and long unused cellar. Great patches of mold clung to the crevices. The stone floor was slippery with an accumulation of black moss, and there was a continual dripping of water from the roof.

The black smoke from Wattanooka's faggot spread in low streamers around the men. There was so little vitality in the air that the men were forced to breathe heavily, and the flame from the faggot threw only a weak glare into their faces. Beyond the limited radius of the light was blackness.

Fallon had been wondering how Wattanooka had chanced to find the particular shaft that led to the room in which Denise had placed him, and now he questioned the Indian.

"Him no hard," was Wattanooka's reply. "You call um 'shaft', eh? All room got shaft. Count shaft, count room from outside. See you stand in window with light. Same in back; same on other side."

The system of subterranean passages was ingenious and had undoubtedly been planned with murder as its sinister purpose. It would be easy for Randall, or any one familiar with the underground passages, to enter any of the various rooms and do away with an unsuspecting or sleeping guest. But Fallon and Wattanooka did not desire to enter any of the unexplored rooms at present.

Fallon especially was interested in the passages themselves, for he now had a conviction that somewhere under the house Lin Underhill was being held captive.

THERE were several smaller tunnels or passages intersecting the main one, and the two men found other shafts that seemed to run upward into the house. But so far as they were able to see at that time, there was no place where Lin Underhill might be concealed.

After they had explored all the passages they found, Wattanooka led Fallon to the mound of rocks at the river bank where he had first entered. They were glad to catch a breath of fresh air, and they climbed out of the tunnel and sat for a while on the rocks at the edge of the river bank, talking over the situation.

By this time Fallon was convinced that Underhill was in one

of the rooms in the house, probably hidden in a secret place known only to Randall himself. He was eager to search the rooms through the shafts that ran from the subterranean passages, but Wattanooka pointed to the sky, eastward, where a streak of gray swam above the horizon. Soon another day would begin.

"No go now," he advised; "wait 'nother night. You like go back to room? Then Wattanooka come here, to-night."

He leaped like a shadow to the dense growth along the river bank, and vanished. Keen of eye though he was, Fallon could not tell in which direction he had gone.

Fallon replaced the rock which Wattanooka had dislodged to enter the tunnel. There were some faggots scattered about, which had probably been brought there by some previous user of the tunnel, and Fallon took several of them with him on his return to the shaft that led to his room.

He had no difficulty in finding the right shaft, nor did he experience any trouble in lifting the hearthstone, and he stepped noiselessly into his room just as dawn was breaking. He replaced the hearthstone, saw that the fastenings of the door leading into the hall were in place, undressed and got into bed.

In his life there had been some strange experiences, but none as strange as he had encountered since reaching the stone house. It seemed incredible that such things could be—that there could be a man like Lumly Randall, relic of the days of the sea rovers; that a man like Denatti could step into this century from the preceding one, or that the stone house itself should be standing in this untracked wilderness.

But here they were—the stone house and its amazing inhabitants. The people were real, because he had met them. The house was real, because he was in it; the subterranean passages were here, because he had been through them. Denise Laville was here, because she had woven a spell about him. And he went to sleep thinking of her.

CHAPTER XX

FORBIDDEN

ONCE AGAIN FALLON'S peculiar sensitiveness to strange sounds awakened him, and he raised his head to listen. The sound was repeated. This time, his senses alert, he discovered that the sound came from the door leading to Denise's room. Her voice, calling him. He leaped out of bed, laid his ear against the heavy planks and whispered the one word: "Denise!"

He heard Denise gasp.

"Oh!" she said. "Are you all right, Fallon?"

"Yes. Are you?"

"Yes. I'm all right. Oh, I'm so glad. I thought something had happened to you. Come in as soon as you can, please. I'll unfasten the door."

Fallon dressed hurriedly, opened the door and saw Denise.

She was standing at one of the windows. Her hair was in neat coils on her shapely head and its lustrous blackness made her fair skin gleam with transparent whiteness in contrast. She wore a dress with a high bodice and an overskirt with soft, drooping flounces; black slippers and a lace scarf. Fallon could not have described her clothing; he was only interested in the beauty of her face.

She placed a finger over her lips to enjoin him to silence, and then stepped close to him and whispered:

"They suspect, I think. Revella insisted that I take my breakfast downstairs this morning. But I defied him. I had Mowaki bring it up, as usual. Mowaki left the door open when he came

123

in and I saw Revella in the hallway. He pretended he wanted to say something to Mowaki, but of course he only wanted to look into my room.

"They are all half-terrorized this morning. They don't want to admit it, but they are. Something terrible happened during the night. A Cree Indian was murdered, with a broken neck. Since this has happened not another Cree will ever enter this house—they could not be dragged in."

With Wattanooka having the run of the secret passages the Crees would be wise to stay out of the house, decided Fallon. Which was well enough.

It had been Revella or Denatti or one of the others who had set the Cree to the task of opening the door, of course, for having searched all the other rooms and finding the outside doors locked or fastened from the inside they would know that Denise had sheltered him.

Whispering, he told her of Wattanooka's visit, how the powerful Indian had entered the room by removing the hearthstone, and what he and Wattanooka had been doing during the night. He then led her into the room, removed his hearthstone, and showed her the dark shaft leading down.

Denise stood beside the shaft and her eyes grew wide with dawning horror. The blood seemed to drain from her cheeks; she closed her eyes and sagged limply forward into Fallon's arms.

Fallon held her tightly. Her lovely head rested on his arm. She had fainted.

And now, holding her so closely, Fallon observed that under her eyes were the dark shadows that are caused by mental agony or worry, and he divined that life in this house for her must be torture. A flood of pity swept over him, and he laid his cheek against hers, reverently caressing her, while he thrilled with an ecstasy so great that he trembled.

HE WAS himself again, however, when a few minutes later he revived her. He had taken her into her own room, where he had placed her in a chair, and he was lightly bathing her face when she opened her eyes, drew a shuddering breath and smiled faintly.

"I am sorry," she said. "I was thinking of the many men who have been murdered in their beds in this house." She shuddered again and covered her face with her hands. When she again looked at Fallon her gaze was steady and her lips firm.

"Are all the rooms in this house like that? Can all of them be entered like that?"

"All."

"Mine also?" She sat erect and stared at the fireplace. The hearthstone was covered with a bear skin. Fallon lifted the rug and glanced at the stone, nodding his head to confirm her fears, although he already knew there was a shaft there.

"Oh!" she exclaimed.

She sat for a time staring straight ahead. She was evidently thinking of the dark deeds she had mentioned, for occasionally she shivered as if a cold wind was striking her.

"It was Lumly Randall!" she said. "Lumly Randall murdered all of them. He was the only one that knew the shafts were there. Even now the others do not know or they would have entered your room that way instead of sending the Cree to open the door."

Fallon nodded. He had reached the same conclusion.

Denise had many questions to ask about the subterranean passages, and she asked them while she and Fallon ate the food that the Japanese had brought for her breakfast. There was more than enough for both.

The necessity of holding their conversation in whispers gave a clandestine appearance and atmosphere to this meeting, which since it was held in Denise's bedroom already suggested intimacy that did not exist. That Denise felt it was apparent from her frequent blushes, but that made her only more charming in Fallon's eyes. It did not occur to him that there could be

another cause for embarrassment, and other reasons for blushing.

Last night, he knew, she had held him off with light banter,
showing him that while she knew of his passion for her she
would not encourage it. She had made it plain to him that she
would never think seriously of a jealous man, and then she had
made him confess that he was jealous. She had slyly poked fun
at him; she had gently ridiculed him, warding off a declaration,
or the possibility of a declaration. She couldn't have made it
plainer to him if she had calmly told him she did not want him.

He wasn't likely to lose his head again. Any woman he might
want would have to want him, also. There would be no half-way
measures with him, and no love that would be all on one side.
He had lost his head when he had caressed her while carrying
her into her room after she had fainted; and he had got a fierce
joy out of that instant, and did not even now regret it.

He sat with his arms folded, staring at the floor. They had
been silent for a time, listening. There was no sound inside the
house.

"Why do you sit and stare at the floor, *m'sieur?*" she said.
"Your name is Jim, isn't it?"

"Yes."

"The floor is interesting, I suppose?"

Bantering him again. He felt she was deliberately amusing
herself and he decided that to-morrow he would join Wattanooka in the forest rather than stay in the house and subject
himself to her gibes. And yet the gibes were gentle ones, and
her voice low and soft.

HE MET her gaze. "Look here," he said. "There's no use in
trying to deceive you. I can see that. You've known since last
night that I love you. I was so eager to see you this morning
that I would have torn the door down to get to you, if necessary.
And you know it. You knew it last night—when I first looked
at you."

"How do you know I knew it?" Her serenity was maddening, but still her voice was gentle. "You loved me then, Jim?"

Fallon laughed. It was a mirthless laugh, though, and in it was the disappointment of the disillusioned who perceives no hope of the fulfillment of his dreams. There was no harshness in it; the laugh was at himself. At his weakness. There was no bitterness.

"Loved you then? Sure. Then and now. Forever. My dear lady, love comes to Jim Fallon only once. It has been rejected, and so it will never again be offered. Can you see now, ma'am, why it should not be made sport of?"

She was calm, but her eyes were very bright. And her voice still gentle—perhaps more gentle than ever. And she laughed in so low a tone that the sound of it could not be heard at the door.

"Is there such a thing as love at first sight, Jim?"

"I always thought people were fools who said there was. Now I am a fool who has experienced it."

"Is it so that there has been no woman in your life, Jim?"

"Women—yes. Love—no."

She frowned. Her lips were pressed tightly together. Her eyes flashed.

"You are not a hypocrite, Jim," she said meditatively. "One needs to look at you only once to know that. But are you the kind of man who would be always faithful to the woman he marries; who would be steady and reliable; who would stay by her side year after year, working and planning and building for her?

"You are an adventurer. You would tire of your wife as you would tire of any place or thing that would tie you down. And when you grew tired of your wife you would have the courage to tell her so. That would be a noble thing to do, Jim, but it would not help your wife any. Isn't that the kind of man you are, Jim?"

"Well, that's the kind of man you seem to think I am," he

answered. "I don't know. I've never taken myself apart like that, but I've a different opinion of myself than you seem to have. I saw you, and I love you. I think I shall always love you. But you don't love me, and that's an end of it."

"I haven't known you quite twenty-four hours yet, Jim."

He smiled wryly.

"It seems like twenty-four years to me," he said.

He faced her now, and his embarrassment was gone. Somehow she had cleared the mental fog that had confused him. Some of the glamour of his enchantment had departed, but in its place was a deeper, purer passion.

He got up, bent over her, and placed his hands on her shoulders, not moving until she looked up and met his gaze. Amazed, she trembled and was silent. His voice was steady.

"Denise," he said, "you are my woman."

He released her, stepped back a little and bowed to her. And while she sat in the chair, watching him, he went into the other room and closed the door behind him.

For a time Denise did not move. Then she got up, fastened the door that Fallon had closed, and stood for a moment, smiling faintly. Then she moved to the mirror and gazed at her reflection in the glass. Her cheeks were aglow, and her eyes were mystic with a light that she had never seen in them before.

Then the smile faded from her lips. For she no longer saw the mirror. She was looking through the mirror at her vision of Fallon's past. Grouped around him were half a dozen women—beautiful women with audacious eyes and alluring smiles, waiting for him to turn and look at them. And Fallon was smiling. He turned his head toward one of the girls....

Denise covered her eyes with her hands.

FALLON did not see Denise again that day. Shortly after his talk with her he slipped into the shaft below the fireplace, drew the hearthstone into place, and descended to the system of tunnels under the house. With lighted faggots he searched the various tunnels and shafts diligently, but could find no place where Underhill might be concealed.

At dusk he went to the end of the tunnel where Wattanooka had left him that morning. He opened the tunnel and climbed to the mound of rocks, first cautiously peering about to see if he was observed. Satisfied that there was no lurking Cree in the vicinity, he worked his way down the rocky bank to the river and drank sparingly of the sparkling water.

The river bed near the mouth of the tunnel was at the base of a clifflike formation of huge rocks, and the great granite slope that led upward to the house began at the top of the cliff, so that Fallon was really at the bottom of a gorge after he had reached the river bed.

The river was not more than twenty or thirty feet wide at this point, and there were breaks in the rock wall on the opposite side where the banks sloped to the water's edge.

It had been into one of these breaks that Wattanooka had vanished when he had left Fallon that morning, and Fallon rather expected the Indian to reappear there out of the tangled brush, to keep his promised appointment. But as Fallon stood there listening, after drinking, he heard no sound to tell him that Wattanooka was coming.

The dusk was yielding to darkness, and he was turning to go back to the tunnel entrance, fearing that he would not be able to find it when the darkness grew deeper, when he saw a broad-bladed caribou spear dart out of the willows on the bank opposite him and come hurtling toward him. The spear fell short. It had traveled slowly, so slowly that it began to fall point first before it reached the middle of the river.

Fallon saw no one. He had thought he had glimpsed a brown arm at the edge of the willows just as the spear was thrown, but he could not be sure. But now the willows were agitated. There came a rustling of leaves, a cracking of twigs. Then silence.

Fallon's gun had leaped into his right hand by the time the

spear had struck the water, but he had vainly scanned the willows for sight of an enemy.

Now he stood, waiting for darkness to come, so that he could return to the tunnel mouth without fear of being seen by an enemy. He waited a full quarter of an hour, and then as nothing happened and the bed of the river became swathed in blackness, he climbed the rocks, found the tunnel opening, and prepared to descend. Poised on the edge of the opening, he heard a gruff, "Ugh, Fallon," from the black void at his right, and he waited, having recognized the voice as Wattanooka's.

And then the Indian was at his side, and they sat for a moment, whispering their greetings. Wattanooka laughed low. "Spear of Cree too short."

"You saw that?" Fallon was amazed. Yet now he knew why the spearman had failed in his cast. Wattanooka had been near. "You got him, eh?"

"Get um heap. Grab um arm. Break um neck. Take um back to Cree village. Show um Wattanooka 'round." He laughed again, adding: "Cree find um in morning. Him no tell about tunnel."

Wattanooka's twelfth Cree. And more terror in the Indian village. Sitting there at the mouth of the tunnel, Fallon expressed his apprehension that Lin Underhill might die of starvation before they should find him. Denise had told him that Randall alone knew where Underhill was hidden, and Randall, near death, would not be able to disclose his whereabouts to those who would take food to him.

Wattanooka grunted.

"Ugh," he said. "We find. To-night, mebbe. Hunt in rooms."

The two friends sank into the mouth of the tunnel, and the heavy rock was dropped into place, sealing them in.

CHAPTER XXI

THE COUNCIL OF WAR

IN A BIG ROOM in the eastern wing of the house, that night, Meeson was sitting on the edge of a great four-poster bed, watching Lumly Randall. Standing near him were Denatti and a man whom Meeson occasionally addressed as Mortwell.

Seated in a chair near a front window was Revella. He was not looking out of the window, for it was black outside. He was leaning back in the chair with his arms folded over his chest and his chin lowered, watching Randall. From where he sat he could see Randall's face. His one eye was closed, and he was breathing stertorously. His face was ashen, his heavy jowls were flaccid, his mouth was open. A great bandage covered his forehead and ran around to the back. He seemed to be near death.

Two other men were in the room—the Japanese, awaiting orders with an expressionless face; and standing near the head of the bed, Goodhull, the colorless individual who had been in the big room downstairs with Revella when Fallon had been admitted by Randall.

Goodhull's eyes were glowing with contradictory emotions—malice and anxiety. It was plain that he hated Randall and wanted him to die, yet hoped he might live for a while.

There was no woman in the room. There had been no woman except Denise in this house since Randall's Indian woman had died about a year ago. Meeson's hands had been the gentlest ones that had touched Randall during his illness. And Meeson's touch was not as gentle as it should have been. Meeson's interest in keeping Randall alive was the interest all of them had in him—to rouse him long enough to force him to tell them where he had hidden Lin Underhill.

The lust for gold was in the veins of all of them. Their hard faces were avid with greed and sharp with impatience.

"How is he, Doc?" asked Revella.

"Looks like the fool is done for," answered Meeson. "But it will be three or four days before I can tell. There's a chance, but it's a mighty slim one. That Fallon man certainly went into him hard."

"You mean you can tell in three or four days whether he will live or not?" questioned Revella.

"That's it."

"What will happen to him after that, if he's going to get well?"

"Chances are that even if he does improve he won't be able to talk for a week."

"By that time Underhill will have starved to death," said Denatti.

"Well, what are we going to do about it if he does?" snapped Meeson. "There's nothing I can do for the damned fool. I didn't bust his head."

"It's a good thing for you that you didn't," said Denatti.

"It is, eh? Well, what would you have done if I had busted it?"

"I'd have let the wind out of a fat doctor."

"Why didn't you let the wind out of Fallon?" sneered Meeson. "He certainly gave you enough provocation. You ain't half as good-looking as you were."

"Stow that gab!" growled Revella. "That don't get us any-where. We've got to find Underhill or change our anchorage. We've been here about a year, waiting for Randall to get some-thing started. I'm getting tired of it. Even after we got this break, we couldn't get a word out of Underhill; and now Randall's dragged him off, and we can't find him. And Randall's got his head busted and can't talk. Can't you give him a shot of something that will make him talk, Doc?"

Meeson shook his head.

THERE was a long silence, during which all eyes were directed at Lumly Randall, who continued to breathe heavily, unaware of the presence of his friends.

"We've had Underhill in the house for months," said Goodhull. "We ought to have got something out of him by this time."

No one paid any attention to Goodhull.

But Goodhull went on: "And now it looks like we never will get anything out of him. What do you suppose that man Fallon came here for? Are there any of you damn fools enough to think that Blandin sent him here? And if Blandin did send him, how does it come that that Indian, Wattanooka, is here, too? Where is Fallon? And where is Wattanooka? They are both in the house, I tell you! They must be! Every night we have seen that the doors were barred!"

"They found another Cree with a broken neck to-night," Revella said. "Wattanooka's mark was on him. They found him at the edge of the Indian village. The Crees are ready to break and run. There are two things we've got to do. We've got to find Underhill, and we've got to kill that neck-breaker, or the Crees will leave us, and we won't be able to muster enough men to drive Hammond's Indians out of Mercie Valley."

Denatti smiled. "Good advice. Certainly, all we have to do is to kill the neck-breaker and find Underhill. But what about Fallon? If he had left us, he would have taken his pack with him. The reasonable conclusion is that he is still in the house. Revella talked to Denise last night at her bedroom door. Revella told us that he saw no signs of Fallon in her room. But Revella sent the Cree to enter the room adjoining Denise's. Did Revella think Fallon was in that room or did he have another purpose in hanging around Denise's bedroom door?"

Revella leaped to his feet. A knife flashed into his hand, but the flash of his dark eyes was more sinister than the weapon.

Denatti's sword hissed as it was drawn from the scabbard.

But Mortwell and Goodhull and Meeson were between the men, and Meeson produced a pistol.

"No more of this damned foolishness!" he said coldly. "You've heard Randall say that if anything happened to him he would depend upon me to run this house for him. And I'm running it!

"I know how it's been with you two jealous fools for a long while. You know what Lumly Randall thinks of you as possible lovers of his ward. Bah! If Randall was himself now he'd tear the gizzards out of you! Revella, or you, Denatti, might camp outside of the girl's room for a thousand years. Much good it would do you. She'd go out by a window rather than look at you. Put those stickers away or I'll blow your heads off!"

Sullenly, and glowering at each other with murderous hate, the men put their weapons away. It was evident that Meeson intended to rule until Randall recovered.

DENATTI was first to leave the room, and he went out backward, smiling mockingly at Revella, who pretended to ignore him. There was a light in the hallway, and Denatti, after he had gone a dozen feet, looked back at the doorway as though fearful that he was being followed.

The Japanese was next to emerge. He went down the dimly lighted hall to a rear stairway, and he, too, glanced fearfully behind him.

When Mortwell appeared he hesitated in the doorway and glanced both ways. Then, tiptoeing, he made his way westward, toward the stairway in that direction, glancing apprehensively at each door he passed, as if expecting a dreadful apparition to emerge. He had to descend to the big room to reach his sleeping quarters in the west wing of the house, and when the light from the bracket lamp in the big room shone upon him his face was pale and his eyes were wide with fright.

He scuttled through the big room and into the next, where he took a candle from a shelf. His hands were trembling so that he had great difficulty in holding the sulphur match to the wick, and in the greenish-yellow light from the match his face was drawn and lined.

He finally got the candle going and glided away in the darkness, reaching the stairs and going up them with a nervous and jerky motion that several time almost extinguished the flame.

At the top of the stairs, in the hallway, he halted. The great, gloomy passageway was so black that the rays from his candle penetrated only a few feet, thereby intensifying the darkness beyond. It had been Mortwell who only this morning had discovered the dead Cree in the hallway. The Cree was lying on his back, but his head had been twisted around until the back of it was uppermost.

Mortwell was thinking of the Cree as he reached the door of his room and inserted the key into the lock. His back was toward the door as he fumbled with the key, and when the door swung open under his eager pushing he fairly leaped inside.

Goodhull did not go out until Meeson left Randall's room, and then he stepped only just outside the door and cringed against the wall until Meeson joined him. Meeson glanced at Goodhull and then up and down the hall.

"Where's the rest of the boys?" he asked.

"Revella and—"

"No. Killen and Atkins and Eccles. And Mortwell. Mortwell was just here. Where did he go?"

"To bed, I suppose."

Meeson laughed harshly.

"Hiding in their rooms, eh? Scared stiff by that neck-breaker. You go hunt up the others and bring them to my room. We're going to make a search for Underhill. We've got to move fast. Randall ain't going to get over this."

Goodhull's face blanched; he trembled, and cringed under Meeson's derisive eye.

"You too!" Meeson said contemptuously. "What a brave, reckless gang of cutthroats you are! Scared of a damned Indian! I'll find him myself."

MEESON stepped past Goodhull and started down the hallway toward the stairs. Goodhull watched him an instant, them fled in the opposite direction. As he ran down the hall he was drawing a key from a pocket. He opened a door and slipped into his room by the time Meeson reached the head of the stairs.

At the bottom of the stairs Meeson took a candle from a shelf and held a match to it.

He did not linger in the big room, nor in the darkened room adjoining it on the west. And he went up the stairs, casting rapid glances behind him. And the candle in his hand was jerking violently. He was as frightened as the others; his talk with Goodhull had been made merely to reassure himself.

His room was at the end of the upstairs hallway, and he lost no time reaching the door. He was inserting the key when he heard a shrill, high screech of terror which carried in it a wail of pitiable hopelessness and a consciousness of imminent doom. The screech died in a muffled gurgle that reverberated in wavering, sobbing cadences along the dark walls of the gloomy hallway. There was a short, shuddering silence, and then the sound of a body falling inert—which is like no other sound in the world.

Meeson stood there, candle in hand, staring down the hall. There came no other sound. It seemed to Meeson that there was nothing in the hallway—only blankness and impenetrable darkness. And yet there was something. The weak, yellow beams of the candle blaze finally brought something into view—a shapeless bundle lying on the floor in front of Mortwell's door.

An icy perspiration bathed Meeson. The candle in his hand shook violently, but he finally got the key into the lock of the door. He pushed the door open, jumped into the room, closed the door, dropped the inside fastenings into place, and stood there, listening.

CHAPTER XXII

REIGN OF TERROR

THE PARALYSIS OF horror had gripped Denise. She had
retired early, and was asleep when that fearful scream had
echoed through the hallway. She had jerked the covers over her
head, and in palpitating dread had cowered from a repetition
of the sound. But she did not hear it again, and out of the
confusion of her thoughts finally came the conviction that
Wattanooka was again at work.

His victim this time had not been a Cree Indian. The shriek
had come from the throat of a white man, and she was certain
that the white man was Mortwell.

Lying in the bed, shuddering and trembling, loathing this
house and all of its inhabitants, as she had loathed it from the
day she had first begun to realize its character and the character of the man who owned it, she was on the verge of nervous
hysteria. She wondered how she had endured it this long.

She got up, lit a candle and sat in a chair with her nightrobe
around her, wondering and listening. She got out of the chair
after a while, unfastened the door to the adjoining room and,
with the candle in hand, peered cautiously into it.

She knew Fallon was not there—she had not heard him.
Fallon and Wattanooka were searching the house for Underhill,
and she was certain that Mortwell, or whoever had screamed,
had had the misfortune to come upon Wattanooka in one of
the rooms.

She went back to bed, to sleep fitfully. In the morning she

went down to breakfast, not waiting for Mowaki to bring it to her, for she was curious about the identity of the man who had screamed during the night.

She found Meeson and Denatti and Revella and Goodhull in the big room.

They had breakfasted, and the dishes had not yet been removed. The big front door was open, letting in a flood of bright sunlight and a cool, frost-laden breeze.

Denatti was standing in front of the fireplace, smoking. One side of his face bore a black and blue bruise, but he was still the beau and the dandy, immaculate and sartorially elegant in his conception of the swashbuckling gentleman. He smiled and bowed and threw a mocking glance at Revella, who had been gazing out of the door when Denise appeared, and was now facing the girl and holding himself as rigid as the barrel of a musket.

Goodhull sat in a chair near the door, elbows resting on his knees and his cupped hands supporting his chin. He did not look around when Denise entered the room.

Meeson was sitting at the big table. His elbows were on its top. His chin, also, was in his cupped hands. Meeson stared at Denise without speaking.

Mowaki entered and spoke to Denise as she seated herself at the table. Then the Jap went out.

Denise sensed a tension in the room, and she knew the reason for it. This third killing had affected the men. Their nerves were on edge. They could hold the outward appearance of gentlemen when their fortunes were surging high, but in adversity they became savages.

Denise did not look at Meeson, though she was aware that Meeson was narrowly watching her. She knew that Meeson had never liked her. His treatment of her had been the gruff courtesy of a grudging and enforced politeness. Now that Randall was not able to impose his will upon these men, they would be different.

*Like avenging furies they advanced
through the stone-lined passage.*

"**WELL,** Miss Laville, did you sleep well last night?" said Meeson. His gaze was level.

"I was awakened—what was it? A shriek, a scream; the cry of a man in terrible agony."

"And did you investigate?"

"No, indeed. I was too frightened. Besides, I knew there were men in the house to attend to such things."

Denatti laughed. "Quite right. There were men in the house, but they did not attend. Meeson, you could not expect Mlle. Denise to investigate the cry when you yourself did not investigate until dawn."

Meeson's jaws tightened.

"Don't drive me too far, Denatti!" he warned.

"Denatti will always demand courtesy to the ladies."

"Bah! What would have happened to this particular lady if it had not been that Lumly Randall had warned you?"

Revella laughed unpleasantly.

"Mlle. Laville is not interested in Denatti, Meeson," he said.

Denatti darted a malignant glance at his rival, but bowed to Denise.

"*Mademoiselle* does not permit Revella to speak for her," he answered spiritedly.

Meeson half rose from his chair and glared at the two men. He seemed on the point of hurling himself upon Denatti. But he restrained himself, probably observing that Denatti's hand had strayed toward his sword hilt. Meeson reddened, paled, sat down again.

"Don't forget what I told you last night," he said. "Mlle. Laville wants neither of you. If I mistake not there are other fish in the sea. Fallon, for example. Eh, *mademoiselle?*"

"Do you mean the gentleman who said he was Lumly Randall's guest?" asked Denise calmly.

"None other. I have not seen him. But I understand he is handsome enough to be a favorite with the ladies. Where is he, *mademoiselle?* You took Fallon out of this room after he knocked the devil out of Denatti. What did you do with him? Where did you take him?"

"I took him nowhere, sir. I went immediately to my room."

"Be careful, *mademoiselle!* Lumly Randall is not here to protect you."

"I am not afraid, Meeson."

Meeson's face paled with fury.

"That's just like you, independent, disdainful. You think yourself above us. Why, if I told you what I know about—"

Denise stood up, facing him.

"Save your breath, Meeson," she said. "Lumly Randall has told me what you are so eager to say. My mother was a captive on the Terror. My father and some other men drew lots for my mother, and my father won her. Well, what of that? Do you dare to say that she was not faithful to my father?"

Meeson stared at her. He evidently had not known that the facts of her parentage had been communicated to her by

Randall. But he hated her, and since he could no longer attack her from that direction he attacked from another.

"I am asking you about Fallon, *mademoiselle*. Where is he? Did you take him to your room?"

Denise looked past Meeson. Mowaki was standing in a distant doorway with a tray and dishes. And Denise spoke to him.

"Mowaki," she said, "please bring my breakfast."

She turned, passed Denatti without looking at him, and walked out of the room.

Mowaki followed her, bearing the tray and the dishes. Meeson stepped forward as if to restrain Denise, but a look at Denatti dissuaded him. He sat down, cursing.

"Damn me! I swear that if she stays here long enough I will throw her to the swine!" He glared at Denatti. "Swine like you and Revella!" he added.

Denatti laughed.

"That cannot happen too soon, Meeson."

But from the look that Meeson gave Denatti it was apparent that when the time came it would be Revella, and not Denatti, to whom the pearl would be cast.

CHAPTER XXIII

WALLS HAVE EARS—
AND HANDS

MORTWELL HAD BROUGHT his death upon himself. For when he had entered his room with the candle in front of him, and had stood with his back against the closed door, the candle-light had revealed to him the giant figure of a half-naked Indian.

The Indian was Wattanooka. He was about to descend the fireplace shaft, after searching the room, when he heard Mortwell at the door. He caught Mortwell's wild, amazed gaze, saw Mortwell draw a knife. He leaped. The candle dropped as Mortwell lunged with the knife. The long blade flashed in the dying candlelight, and Mortwell's wrist was gripped and twisted. The knife dropped, striking Mortwell's leg and landing on the tip of the handle, with little sound. Mortwell wrestled and struck viciously with his fists. When he felt an arm go around his neck, felt the ironlike muscles begin to tighten, he knew what impended and he emitted the shriek that had palsied Meeson.

After tossing Mortwell's body into the hall, Wattanooka closed the door and barred it. He picked up his torch, let himself into the shaft, slid the hearthstone into place and descended. He and Fallon were searching all the rooms for Underhill, Fallon utilizing the shafts on one side of the subterranean passage, Wattanooka the other side. Wattanooka so far had been in three rooms and had found them all unoccupied except Mortwell's. He entered a half dozen others before he joined Fallon in the passage below.

In the light from the pine torches the Indian's face had the cold hardness of the stoic, and yet his eyes were gleaming with a strange fire.

"No find um yet?" he questioned. "Ugh. Me no find um, too. Find other man—think Mortwell. Killum. Put um in hall. Revella find um, mebbe. Revella know Wattanooka here. Some time Wattanooka find Revella in room...."

"Mortwell, eh?" said Fallon. His face was grim. He stood in the glare of the firebrands, the soot from the smoke flecking his cheeks. His hair was in wild disorder; he was covered from head to foot with cobwebs, dirt and dust.

Standing together, the red man and the white, with the black smoke from the torches swirling and eddying around them and the ragged rock walls and roof of the subterranean passage closing them in, they made a picture of primitive force and strength that might have interested even the Roman gladiators.

The picture might have interested Revella, even more. For it was upon Revella that the Indian's thoughts were centered as he stood there with Fallon. It had been Revella who had driven a knife into Wattanooka's side that day at Big Tree portage, and it had been Revella who had helped to inflict the torture upon Adam Hammond, whom Wattanooka had loved.

Revella was not found that night. Nor Underhill. When the dawn broke the two men were at the tunnel entrance breathing the air of the outside world. And before the sun rose they had closed the mouth of the tunnel and were far southward, in the forest, asleep in a shelter they had erected. For Wattanooka would not sleep in the house, and Fallon was glad to get away from its damp walls, its gloomy atmosphere.

But when darkness came again they resumed their search for Underhill. They were unsuccessful that night and the following night, although they searched all the rooms and the towers. The search of the rooms they conducted in the first hours of the night, while the occupants were absent. The remainder of the night they devoted to a careful scrutiny of the

walls of the tunnel and of the various other tunnels that intersected or branched off from the main tunnel.

A dozen nights passed in this fashion. Then Fallon returned
to the room that Denise had given him.

HE MADE no sound as he swung himself out of the shaft, for
he did not want Denise to know that he had returned. He was
in no mood to talk with her, to endure looking upon her loveliness when he knew she was not for him. He was not a man
to pursue women or to force himself upon them. He was not
adept at love-making. When he had told her that she was his
woman he had meant that she was the only woman he had ever
loved.

He was after the pack that he had left lying on the floor of
the big room on the night Lumly Randall had opened the door
for him. He did not know where he might find it, but he meant
to get it. For soon, if he did not find Lin Underhill, he would
leave the house, to search for him in the surrounding forests.
For he was beginning to entertain a conviction that Randall
had taken Underhill away.

Wattanooka was in the tunnel, searching. Wattanooka did
not believe that Underhill had been taken away. Each time that
Fallon had suggested the possibility, the Indian had vigor-
ously disagreed.

Fallon did not replace the hearthstone, for he intended to
return this way after finding his pack. His moccasined feet made
no sound as he moved to the hall door, lifted the fastenings,
opened the door and stepped out into the hallway.

There was no light. In the blackness, Fallon guided himself
to the stairway by feeling his way along the stone wall. There
was no light downstairs, and he went down the stairway and
into the room where he had first seen Denise by cautiously
sidling along the walls and through the doorways. When he
reached the door that led into the big room he paused and
listened. There was no sound anywhere, and so he felt his way
along the wall to a point near the front door.

There, near the wall, on the floor, he came upon the pack. He ran his hands over it to identify it. No one had disturbed it. The rifle was still under the straps. He swung it to his shoulders, slipped his arms through the straps and began the return trip. He made the trip without incident, and after he let himself into the door of the room Denise had given him he noiselessly placed the pack on the floor near the shaft and prepared to go down.

The pack was awkward to handle. He intended to lower it into the shaft and work it down ahead of him. But the barrel of the rifle somehow got crosswise and struck an edge of stone, creating a sharp, rasping sound. It was the first noise he had made and it brought an instant response.

The door leading to Denise's room slowly opened. First a candle, and then Denise's head and face and shoulders, appeared. Fallon got an impression that she had been standing at the door, listening. Perhaps, previously, he had made a sound that had awakened her. Or perhaps she had not yet gone to bed. It did not matter; she was here.

Her eyes were big and bright, and a bit resentful, as she stepped into the room. The flame of the candle in her hand disclosed Fallon kneeling at the edge of the shaft, his face and body covered with cobwebs and dust. His forty-five Colt had leaped into his right hand at the sound of the door being opened. He shoved the weapon back into its holster, rested the pack on the floor, and got to his feet to face her.

She was dressed in garments that made her look like a boy. Knee-length trousers, a mackinaw coat, a cap, leggings, moccasins, woolen shirt. Sight of her again did something to Fallon—swelled his lungs, sent a sharp pang of longing through him.

Her gaze rested first upon Fallon and then upon the pack, with the rifle sticking between the straps. Her eyes widened a little, then narrowed with mockery.

"MONSIEUR FALLON is leaving us?" she whispered. "Is Lin Underhill found?"

"He isn't in the house," answered Fallon. "We think he is hidden somewhere in the forest."

She shook her head.

"Underhill is somewhere in the house or under it," she said. "I thought you and Wattanooka had gone," she added. There was reproach in her eyes.

"We shall not go until we have found Lin Underhill. And when we go you may go with us, if you care to do so."

"I think I shall go when you go, *monsieur*. Oh, this terrible, terrible house!"

"What has happened. Tell me, ma'am?"

"Nothing yet, Monsieur Fallon. It is what may happen. I know there have been murders committed here. But while Lumly Randall was able to be around I had no fears for myself. Now I do not know what is going to happen. Revella is growing bolder. Denatti follows me. Meeson looks at me so strangely. And, Monsieur Fallon, you have not been in your room for twelve nights."

Fallon's blood surged mightily. She had noticed his absence from the room she had given him. However, that probably meant very little. She could wish him to be near her in the rôle of protector, merely. He frowned.

"Very well. I shall sleep in the room hereafter," he told her.

She seemed relieved. She smiled.

Fallon was amazed at the sudden change in her. Her manner was no longer doubtful or reproachful. The troubled light had gone from her eyes. Fallon caught a flash from them that made him tremble for an instant, so that he had to clench his hands to keep from taking her in his arms.

"Why are you dressed like that?" he asked gruffly, to keep her from discovering his passion.

"I had got ready to search for Monsieur Fallon," she declared.

"Why?" he asked.

"To see if he had found Underhill," she said.

"You were going to descend to the tunnel?"

"Why, yes; of course. Underhill is not in any of the rooms, therefore he must be under the house."

"You'd better go back to bed," he told her.

She smiled at him with tantalizing calmness.

"Monsieur," she said, "is that the way you are going to speak to your wife—if you get one?"

"I shall never have a wife."

"Then you will be very lonely, Monsieur Fallon."

He did not answer; he was again lowering the pack. He dropped it a little distance and then found the rungs of the ladder and descended until only his head and shoulders were in the room.

Denise was watching him, smilingly. "I am going to follow you down the ladder."

"You will not."

"I will! I should have gone if you had not come to-night, Monsieur Fallon."

"You are obstinate—like all women."

"Ah! I presume Monsieur Fallon knows a great deal about women?"

"A little. Enough to perceive that you are going to dominate the man you marry."

"The man I marry will do things for me, cheerfully, *monsieur.*"

Fallon sighed. One thing was certain—he would not be the man she would marry. She would not be mocking him if there were any hope for him.

"Well," he said, "come on, if you are determined. I will go down with the pack and wait in the tunnel until you join me. Then I will come back and replace the hearthstone."

FALLON went down. When he reached the bottom he set the pack down at a little distance from the foot of the ladder, lighted a pine torch and held it above his head to light Denise's way. She came down lightly and rapidly, and in a moment was standing beside him. Her eyes were wide with wonder, but she gave Fallon a dazzling smile that brought another to his lips.

"That is so much better, *monsieur.*"

"What is better?"

"To see you smile. You are very handsome when you smile."

Flattery and raillery, banter and mockery. Fallon abruptly began to climb the ladder. He had stuck the torch into a crevice in the rock floor of the tunnel. He went up, slid the hearthstone into place, and descended again, to find Denise fearfully watching Wattanooka, who stood a short distance away, his big belt-ax in hand.

Denise's face was pale; it was evident she thought the Indian an enemy. For Wattanooka stood, grim and silent, and stared at her. But when he saw Fallon emerge from the shaft his eyes gleamed with interest and friendliness.

"Ugh," he said. "White woman."

"Wattanooka, this is Denise Laville," said Fallon.

Denise moved forward to the red giant and silently held out her right hand to him. Wattanooka stared incredulously, then took the hand, gripped it, seemed to marvel at its delicacy.

"How," he said.

He looked at Fallon. His black eyes were inscrutable.

"You woman?" he asked.

These were almost Fallon's words, spoken to Denise nearly two weeks ago. Fallon reddened, and said, "No."

"You fool," declared Wattanooka.

Fallon turned away, not caring to meet Denise's gaze at that moment.

However, Wattanooka met it. And what Wattanooka saw in the girl's eyes caused his own to twinkle with sympathy and understanding and secret satisfaction.

CHAPTER XXIV

A PIRATE'S REVENGE

WHILE WATTANOOKA AND Fallon and Denise were searching the underground passages, Meeson and Revella were in Randall's room. Denatti and the others had gone out only a few minutes before, and Meeson had closed the door after them, and locked it. Then for a few minutes he stood at one of the windows of the room, peering out into the darkness. A new moon was swimming low over the eastern horizon, and sections of the dark forest were disclosed to Meeson. After a time he went to the bed, where he stood, watching the sick man.

Randall's face was flushed. There were great blue veins in his forehead that seemed on the point of bursting. His one eye was wide open. It was not the eye of sanity, for it was wild and uncomprehending. It quested here and there as if in search of something that was not to be found. It glared at Meeson and Revella with no recognition, but with a dazed, insensate light— passion which could not be concentrated or directed; the chaos of a brain that was no longer capable of separating fact from fantasy, the real from the unreal.

Randall's huge body was in constant motion. His legs and arms were jerking. His great head, still bandaged, rolled from side to side, and his chest heaved as he fought for breath.

Meeson watched him calmly, with steady malice; but Revella could not be motionless for an instant. He walked back and forth in the room, always keeping his gaze upon Randall, as if expecting him to leap from the bed.

And it seemed that such a determination was uppermost in Randall's mind.

But if Meeson feared that Randall would get out of bed he gave no sign. His interest in Randall appeared to be professional, except for the malice in his gaze.

"There's no hope, Revella," he said, over his shoulder. "Randall is through. We are going to have a crazy man on our hands."

"Hell!" exclaimed Revella.

"I expect paralysis, too," continued Meeson. "He won't be able to move. That means we'll have to wait on him. I'll be damned if I'll do it. I'm going to give him a shot of strychnine."

"That won't do, Meeson. We've got to keep him alive if we want to find Underhill."

"Underhill has starved to death by this time. It's been over two weeks since Randall got his head broke." Meeson looked at Revella and there was a wild, furtive glare in his eyes.

"I'm going to get away from this damned house!" he declared. "That big Indian is here. The doors and windows are locked every night, but still he gets in. He was in Mortwell's room. Mortwell was in his room when he yelled, that night. He was dumped into the hall from his own door. And the next morning we find the door locked, from the inside. I'm getting the creeps. I don't sleep any more. I'm getting jumpy. Blazes! Think of waking up some night and seeing that red devil bending over you? Think of opening the door of your room and seeing him standing close to you? The Crees are ready to stampede. But Mortwell wasn't a Cree, Revella. He was a white man."

Revella laughed cynically, but his face was pale.

"Bah!" he exclaimed. "You're like the Crees, Meeson. Because there was the mark of a moccasin on the neck of the Cree I sent up there to get into Denise's spare room, you think Wattanooka killed him. The Crees say that is Wattanooka's mark, all right, but after what we did to Wattanooka at Big Tree I doubt if he could break a child's neck. We took a lot of the strength out of him there, Meeson. Wattanooka isn't here. It's

Fallon. And there's nothing mysterious about him being in the house. He's a good-looking man and Denise has appropriated him. She had him hid somewhere."

"The hussy. She'd do that. But it doesn't sound reasonable, Revella. Fallon told Randall that Blandin had sent him here."

"YOU SWALLOWED Fallon's story, eh?" Revella sneered. "Well, I don't. And Randall didn't swallow it. Mowaki just told me he saw what happened the night Randall was hurt. Randall heaved a knife at him, but Fallon jumped over the table and landed with both feet on Randall's chest. Now what happened before Randall threw the knife? Simple, Meeson. Randall discovered that Fallon was an impostor."

"Why didn't Mowaki tell us this before?" roared Meeson.

Revella grinned crookedly.

"He was told not to tell, I suppose. Denise took Fallon with her to her room that night, after Randall went down. Mowaki saw them go. It was only yesterday that I got it out of him."

"Who instructed him not to tell about it?"

"Denise. She told him that Fallon had gone away."

Meeson's face purpled.

"Damn Mowaki!" he almost shouted. "I'll tear him apart!"

Meeson's rage was great, and yet he seemed relieved. The news that Fallon had gone was welcome. He was glad that there was no foundation for his fears that Wattanooka was in the house.

His rage now took a new turn. It centered upon Denise. Denise had harbored Fallon. He had never liked her. He had resented her presence in the stone house. And now she had betrayed them all.

"Damnation!" he shouted "I'll fix her! I'll choke her lying tongue out!"

Behind Meeson, Randall was in the grip of a mighty passion. His breath was coming with a shrill rasping sound, his solitary eye was rolling so that only the white was visible; his muscles were heaving and straining and his arms were beating the quilts. He was striving to get out of the bed. He was muttering unintelligibly.

Revella peered at him. Revella's face blanched; he smirked and stepped in front of Meeson so that he could not be seen by Randall's eye.

"Does that big swab hear us?" he asked.

Meeson looked over his shoulder at Randall. There was amazement in his glance. But he spoke contemptuously.

"There's more life in him than I thought. Yes; I think he understands. Little good it will do him."

A new mood seized Meeson. The malice that had been expressed in his manner toward Randall now manifested itself. He went to the bed, sat upon its edge, gripped Randall's arms and held them down while he whispered into the stricken man's ear:

"Listen, Randall. You've bullied me for thirty-five years. You've cheated me out of more than one share of what belonged to me. I've got you now, where I can get even with you. Do you know what I am going to do? Denise. Do you understand? Denise Laville. The girl you've taken such good care of. The girl you have protected. The girl you have always claimed is descended from a royal line. The daughter of a nobleman's daughter! Do you know what I am going to do with her? I am going to turn her over to Revella. Revella! Do you understand? Revella—ha, ha, ha! Revella is going to take her to his cabin up north! Now, damn you, think of that! You understand, eh?"

A white froth appeared upon Randall's lips; his mouth was working soundlessly, and his huge and flaccid jowls were agitated by the jerking of the neck cords under them. His eye had ceased rolling; it glared fixedly, with hideous malignance, with deadly hate and fury, at Meeson.

"He's going to get up!" There was a ring of terror in Revella's voice. He darted to the hall door and stood there with a hand

upon the latch, ready to escape from the room should his pre-
diction prove true.

Meeson laughed

"Take it easy, Revella. He won't get up. He's crazy, but I think
he understood what I said to him. Partly, anyhow. Don't worry
about his getting up. He's paralyzed—the nerve centers. Now
that he knows what is going to happen to Denise, we'll leave
him alone for two or three days to think it over. Nice prospect
for him, eh?"

Meeson stood, grinning broadly at Randall. And Randall,
lying perfectly still, glared back at him. After a while, when it
appeared that Meeson's mirth was appeased, he abruptly turned
to the door and went out of the room, Revella following him.

THEY went downstairs to the big room, lit a candle and seated
themselves at the big table, before a stone flagon of wine and
glasses. For a while they talked and drank, and then Meeson
drew out a pocket medicine case and selected a phial which he
passed over to Revella for inspection.

"Dope," he said. "There's just enough in there to knock her
out for twenty-four hours. I don't know how you are going to
get her to take it. That's your affair. A light wine will disguise
the taste; or coffee, or any strongly flavored liquid or food. Don't
be in too big a hurry. Don't try to take her out of the house in
the daytime. To-morrow night, maybe, so the Crees won't see
you. They're crazy about her, you know, and they'd likely interfere. How are you going to get her up there?"

"Canoe. There's only one portage—a short one."

"You'll marry her, eh?" suggested Meeson.

"No man will take her without marriage, Meeson. She'd kill
herself. I'll be glad to marry her. I've wanted to, but she wouldn't
have me. She'll have to marry me when I get her up there. I'll
send to the factor at Churchill and he'll tie the knot."

"I don't care what you do with her," declared Meeson. "You
can take her up the river and drown her." A new thought struck

him and he glared at Revella. "I wonder if she knows where Underhill is?"

Revella shook his head with a quick negative.

"Hell, no. She'd have been feeding him. I've watched her; she hasn't left her room in a week."

"Well, get her out of here before that gang from the coast gets here. They ought to be here to-morrow. Blandin, too. If you get her out of the house before Blandin gets here I'll tell him Randall sent her to the coast, to ship out. The news will please that big slob, too. He's just about wild about her."

Revella's teeth gleamed. He got up, stretched himself, looked at Meeson. His eyes were glittering with eagerness.

"I'm going to bed," he said. His gaze swept the room. He started, stood rigid, stared. His voice caught in his throat, then burst out hoarsely:

"Fallon's pack! It's gone! I saw it there to-night, Meeson. Fallon is still in the house!"

Meeson had jerked abruptly around to face the corner where the pack had been. His face whitened; he leaned against the table as if for support. His breath came shrilly.

After a while, when the shock had passed, Meeson spoke.

"You were right, Revella; she's hiding him. In her room."

Revella's face flamed with sudden passion. He drew a long knife from a sheath at his belt, under his coat, and, without glancing again at Meeson, went through the west door, which would take him up the stairs and into the upper hallway that led to Denise's room.

And Meeson, after watching Revella go through the west door, got up, smiled slyly, and went through the east door to the stairs that led up to Randall's room. Meeson paused at Randall's door and listened. A low moaning greeted him—the sound of a man in mortal agony; a strange whining and mewing; a gibbering voice that begged and pleaded and cursed.

CHAPTER XXV

TRICKED

REVELLA, LISTENING AT Denise's door in the hallway upstairs, heard no sound from the room. Jealousy, aroused by Meeson's reference to Fallon, had driven Revella to his action in spying upon Denise, but his vigil outside the door brought him no satisfaction. He could not even hear Denise breathing, and therefore he concluded she was in a soundless sleep. Nor did Revella hear any sounds through the door next to Denise's—the door of the spare room.

He had told Meeson that Wattanooka was not in the house, but through the long hours from the time he reached the hallway until daylight began to filter into the gloomy corridor, Revella was bathed in an icy perspiration. Every slight sound startled him; the blackness that surrounded him was filled with frightful images that leered at him.

With his long knife clutched tightly in his hand he waited and listened; and several times he was certain he could dimly see Wattanooka's giant figure taking shape in the shadows. He was afraid, and yet his passion sustained him. At dawn, though, he silently stole away and went to his room in the east wing.

Not more than half an hour later the hearthstone of the fireplace in the room adjoining Denise's slowly lifted. It was slid back and Fallon's head and shoulders appeared in the opening. He swung himself lightly upward, then reached a hand down and helped Denise out of the shaft. Fallon's face was grim and dirty, but, in some miraculous manner, Denise had escaped both dust and grimness. For after Fallon helped her from the shaft she stood, looking at him, her fair skin white and flawless, her eyes half smiling at him.

"That was a wonderful adventure, M. Fallon," she declared.

"Failure again."

"Yes. But it is not your fault. You have tried. You will keep on trying until you find him."

"Of course. That's what I'm here for. Lin's father is depending on me."

"Gail Hammond is depending upon you too, *monsieur*. Do you remember when you left Wattanooka and myself in the main tunnel while you went to inspect another? Well, while you were gone Wattanooka told me about Gail. She must be a beautiful girl."

"She is."

"She loves Lin Underhill."

"So she says."

"Did you fall in love with her, Jim?"

"No."

"Why? You like beautiful women."

"Look here," he said gruffly; "I don't fall in love with every good-looking woman I see."

She suddenly looked up at him and smiled. Then she turned from him and peered into her room. She shivered and turned to face him again. Her face was serious.

"You will sleep here?" she asked.

"No. I'm going to go into the timber with Wattanooka. We are going to search outside for Underhill."

She shivered again.

"You will come back again, to-night? I am afraid, *monsieur*. I have a strange feeling—a fear. I do not know what it is."

"I'll leave the hearthstone off. I'll be back here before dark. If anybody tries to force the door, go down the shaft and go through the big tunnel toward the river."

She entered her room, smiling at Fallon, who descended the shaft.

DENISE slept fitfully, restlessly. But at last she must have fallen into a deep slumber, for she heard nothing until she was awakened by a step in the hall. She sat up and observed that the sun was in the west. She got up, dressed, and went to a window.

She saw Denatti getting into a canoe at the little wharf. He did not see her, and she watched him seat himself, push off, and begin to paddle down the stream toward the Cree village. From the window she had a good view of the village, and she was certain she saw Goodhull there, and Eccles, and the other men—Atkins and Killen. They often visited the village, and she supposed Denatti was going there too.

The step she heard must have been Meeson's. He'd been to his room, she supposed, which was to the right of the head of the stairs. She made up her bed. Then she dropped into a chair and sat there listening. She was afraid to go downstairs for food. But she wasn't hungry, for in the tunnel during the night Wattanooka had produced food that he had appropriated from the kitchen. He did not tell her how he had obtained it, but his eyes had glinted with satisfaction when she had taken some of it.

Presently she again heard footsteps. They came up the stairs, down the hall. There was no stealth in them; the sound they made was clear and sharp. She expected them to go down the hall, but they stopped at her door.

A sharp knock, that somehow expressed a demand. Then a voice—Revella's.

"Denise!" he called. "Come! Hurry!"

Startled, she ran to the door and called through it:

"What is it, please?"

"Denise, it's Randall. He's in bad shape. He's going to die. He's calling for you. I think he's got something to say to you. Hurry!"

It had come at last. He wanted to tell her about her mother, as he had been promising to do for years. Swiftly she unfastened the door and stepped into the hall, leaving the door partly open. Revella was waiting for her. The light in the hall was dim and she could not see Revella's face clearly. In fact she had no opportunity, for when Revella saw her he turned quickly and began to walk down the hall toward the stairs.

She followed him down. They went through the lower rooms, crossed the big room. The door of the big room was open, and through it she saw that the sun was low; that its rays, turning golden, were tinting the leaves of the trees.

She followed Revella up the stairs of the east wing and stood beside him as he opened the door of Randall's room. Once inside she had no interest in Revella, for she knew from Randall's appearance that a crisis had come.

He was lying flat on his back. His legs and arms were jerking with spasmodic motions, and he was muttering as his head turned from side to side.

Denise saw the froth on his lips; the purple veins on his forehead that seemed ready to burst; his solitary eye, which was rolling wildly. The sight appalled her. Her face blanched, she swayed and held tightly to one of the bedposts.

And then Revella was at her side offering her a small glass filled with a dark liquid.

"It is terrible, Denise. I did not want to call you, but he insisted. Drink this wine. It will fortify you for what is to come."

She took the glass from Revella, drank half its contents. It seemed at first to stimulate her. But as she stood there it seemed that the room began to whirl slowly. The bed appeared to recede; a strange nausea oppressed her. She felt Revella's arms slip around her; she saw Revella's face close to hers. She struggled a little.

CHAPTER XXVI

DUEL

STANDING THERE, HOLDING the unconscious girl in his arms, Revella grinned into Randall's eye, which had ceased rolling. The eye was opened so wide that it appeared about to pop out of its socket. It glared with hate unutterable, with comprehension.

Revella swung Denise into his arms and carried her to the door. She was a limp burden and not heavy, so Revella had no difficulty in unfastening the door and opening it. He did not bother to lock it, but as he stepped out into the hall he glanced up and down to see if he was observed.

Revella had chosen the time well. There was no one in the house except Randall, Meeson, Denise and himself. Meeson had gone to his room; he was through, getting ready to leave the house. He was going to take an Indian guide and go to Churchill, where he would wait for a ship to take him back to civilization. But before he left he meant to administer strychnine to Randall.

Randall was helpless, Meeson was in his room, and so there was no one to spy upon Revella. There was plenty of time. Dusk had not yet come, but he could carry Denise through a rear door, keeping the house between him and the Cree village until he reached the canoe which he had concealed in some willows a little distance up the river. In the canoe were supplies that would last until he reached his cabin.

When he reached the big room Revella paused in the

doorway. He had forgotten his sheath knife—a long-bladed weapon which he wore suspended from a belt around his waist. It was in his room, and he would have to return for it. He could get it and return to the room while he could count a hundred.

He thought first of taking Denise with him, but decided to leave her in the big room. He looked at the great, brass-bound sea chest that stood against the east wall, but chose the table and gently placed Denise upon it. Then he ran through the east doorway and up the stairs to his room, which was at the farther end of the hallway. He got the knife, quickly strapped the belt around his waist, and ran down the stairs. But at the door of the big room he stopped short, and stood with his hands against the jambs, staring in consternation.

Standing beside the table, close to Denise, was Denatti.

His muscles rigid, every nerve jumping, Revella's senses grasped several things quickly. The front door had been open. Now it was closed. The fastenings were not in place; the door might be opened from the outside. Denatti had his sword at his side.

Twilight had come; the sun had gone down. Denise had not stirred. Her right hand, white and shapely, was dangling over the edge of the table, the wrist partly hidden by some filmy white lace at the end of the black sleeve of her dress. Denatti knew what was happening. His face was pale, his lips were in straight lines except for a slight curve of contempt at one of the corners; his eyes were cold, hard, and agleam with hate.

"So this is why you got the canoe ready?" he said. "I was wondering."

Revella did not answer. There was no need. He and Denatti knew each other only too well.

Revella now realized that he was at a disadvantage. He had not expected interference from Denatti; he had seen Denatti paddling down the river and had thought he intended visiting the Cree village. So he had left his rifle and pistol in the canoe, so that he would not be hampered with them while carrying

Denise. He had been so eager to get away that he had almost forgotten his knife.

THE KNIFE had a long blade, but Denatti's sword had a longer one. And Denatti knew how to use a sword. Moreover, Denatti apparently was aware of the fact that his rival's only weapon was a knife, for he laughed derisively.

"No gun, eh?" he said. He moved away from the table, stepping cautiously backward, keeping one hand on the table edge as if to aid him to leap quickly should such an action be necessary. And as he moved he watched Revella's right hand. For Revella, who was now crouching, had drawn the big knife, and was balancing it in a strange fashion as he followed Denatti.

Denatti, backing away, drew his sword. He knew that Revella was a knife-thrower; that he was amazingly swift and accurate with the weapon. Revella needed only an instant, hardly more than the time that would be consumed in flickering an eyelash, to send the knife flashing to its mark. That was why Denatti was feeling his way along the table. He dared not permit his gaze to wander for the merest fraction of a second.

Denatti knew that if he could draw his enemy to close quarters he would win swiftly, and so his aim was to circle out into the room, away from the table, where a sudden lunge would finish Revella. But Revella, intent upon throwing the knife, had no intention of doing as Denatti wished. He followed Denatti around the table, past the end and down the side nearest the fireplace, alert for a momentary lapse of watchfulness, or an accident that would bring him the opportunity he sought.

There were several chairs along the side of the table. Some of them had been pushed under so that only their backs were visible, but others were in various positions; and all of them presented hazards for Denatti. If he stumbled against one of them, or backed against one in such a position as to prevent his moving quickly, or if he so much as glanced down at one of them, Revella would have him.

But Denatti was cool and careful. He moved backward very

slowly, always watching Revella's right hand. Some prescience seemed to warn him of the position of the chairs behind him, for not once down the entire length of the table did he hesitate. Nor did he back into one of the chairs. Nor did he glance for an instant at Denise, as he passed her. Revella had waited for that, but it did not happen.

When Denatti reached the east end of the table he swung widely outward until one of the great stone columns support- ing the second story was between him and his enemy. Then he laughed.

The laugh goaded Revella. Denatti had anticipated that. Revella came closer, yet not close enough to permit Denatti to make the fatal lunge. But as Revella moved forward, Denatti stepped out from behind the stone pillar and edged toward him, his right side foremost, the blade in his hand weaving and circling.

And now it was Revella that sought distance. He backed as Denatti advanced, and the latter mocked him. Yet Denatti was watchful. He knew what Revella could do with a knife. Denatti dared not rush. He continued to follow Revella. Around the room they went, and then along the side of the table, until they were about where they had been when they started, except that their positions were reversed. And at the end of the table Revella backed against a chair. In moving away from it he upset it. It crashed to the floor as Denatti leaped and lunged.

Denatti had misjudged the distance, or Revella, anticipating the thrust, slid back to evade it. The point of the sword vainly stabbed the air two or three feet from Revella's chest. The knife flashed from Revella's side, so quickly that there was only a glittering line for the eye to follow.

Denatti felt the wind from it. He may have thought it had struck him. He may have been momentarily paralyzed by the suddenness of the movement and his escape. For he stood, motionless, his lips parted. The knife went forward and upward. It struck the ceiling, rang against the beams, and fell with a clang to the stone floor. Before it struck the men were locked in each other's arms, fighting for the sword that was still in Denatti's hand.

REVELLA, slender though he was, was the stronger. He had gripped Denatti's sword arm with his left hand, his right arm was around Denatti's waist as he drove furiously forward, trying to back his enemy against the table edge near where Denise was lying. Denatti, not as strong as Revella, was more active. Twice, realizing that Revella's purpose was to bend him backward over the table, he whirled away.

Whirling, raging, fighting, they struck one of the stone pillars. Denatti's right shoulder bore the unexpected weight and shock. The sword flew from his hand, struck the table top and slid to the floor on the other side. Revella followed it like a hound leaping a fence. He landed on his hands and feet within a foot of the sword, grasped it and got up, gloating.

But Denatti had sped to the knife, and when Revella again faced about, Denatti, with the knife in hand, was retreating toward the front door, evidently meditating flight.

But he had no opportunity to open the door, for Revella was after him, and Denatti was forced along the wall toward the door that opened in the west wall of the room—the door through which Fallon had first seen Denise. This door was closed, also; and it opened inward.

The two men were moving about, cat-footed, noiselessly— Denatti backing away, Revella following. They had passed the hinged side of the door and Revella was crowding Denatti into the recess formed by the corner of the fireplace, when the door creaked and began to open—swinging out into the room so that Denatti and Revella were behind it.

Dusk had come. There was now barely enough light in the room for the enemies to see each other's faces, or to see Denise, lying motionless on the table.

Denatti and Revella stood motionless, waiting. The door opened slowly until it stood straight out into the room. Then a man appeared, stood for an instant looking at Denise and then leaped to her side.

The man was Fallon.

He bent over Denise, whispered her name. In that position he felt a sword's point pressing into his side just above the hip. He turned his head and saw Revella standing behind him. Denatti, knife in hand, was closing the door through which Fallon had entered the room.

CHAPTER XXVII

BARE HANDS AGAINST STEEL

THE APPEARANCE OF a common enemy had brought a temporary truce between Revella and Denatti.

Revella, now certain that it had been Fallon who had killed Mortwell and the two Crees, was eager to take revenge, and he stiffened his muscles to drive the sword blade through Fallon's body. But Denatti, having a grudge to pay, wished to participate in the murder, and so he danced forward, knife in hand, calling upon Revella to withhold the thrust. Reluctantly Revella obeyed, though he did not remove the sword's point from Fallon's side.

Denatti, coming close, deftly plucked the pistol from the holster at Fallon's hip, backed away, placed the weapon on the table out of Fallon's reach, and faced Fallon, to bow and smile at him.

"So Monsieur Fallon did not go away after all," he said coldly. "Monsieur Fallon has stayed to permit Denatti to repay him for that blow."

Fallon had kept his word to Denise and had returned to her room through the shaft at the time appointed, only to find Denise gone and the hall door ajar. He had been in the heavy undergrowth near the entrance to the tunnel half an hour ago, and from there he had seen some white men in the Cree village.

Assuming that there was no one in the house with the exception of Denise, who had probably gone down to the kitchen to order food from Mowaki, he had decided to explore the rooms.

He had gone into several, and then he had entered the big room, to find himself trapped.

He had heard no sound; he did not know that Denatti and Revella had been fighting over Denise. Yet Denise was lying on the big table, unconscious, and Denatti and Revella were in the room with her. From her pallor, which was accentuated by the deepening dusk, he judged she had fainted.

When he had first reached her side, not knowing that any one was in the room with her, the shock of seeing her in that position had bewildered him. But when he had felt the point of the sword at his side and had turned his head to see the two men in the room with him, comprehension came instantly. And with the comprehension came rage.

His gaze rested momentarily upon the revolver that Denatti had taken from him. Denatti observed the glance, darted quickly to the table, snapped open the cylinder, tossed the cartridges upon the floor and hurled the weapon into a corner.

That digression from his original purpose almost lost Denatti his advantage. For Fallon, turning quickly, evaded the thrust of Revella's sword and struck with savage force full at Revella's jaw.

The blow missed Revella's face and struck his shoulder; but Revella staggered, fell, and slid along the floor to a point between the table and the front door, the sword trailing and clanging after him.

Denatti had rushed as Fallon struck, hoping to be able to strike from behind. But Fallon, lighter on his feet than either of the two, had turned and was bounding toward Denatti before Revella had ceased to slide. Although armed with the long knife, Denatti had not the courage to face the charge of the man he had called "lout." He turned, leaped behind the stone pillar nearest him.

Like a huge cat, Fallon was after him.

Denatti knew the possession of the knife would avail him little if Fallon caught him. For Denatti now began to gain some

A brawny red arm was raising the lid of the great sea chest.

conception of the strength and elasticity of the muscles of the man who was after him. The great arms were swinging at his sides, balancing him as he leaped here and there in pursuit; the hands gripping the backs of chairs and hurling them out of the way with as much ease as if they were made of paper, and reaching for Denatti as the latter desperately and ineffectively slashed at him with the knife.

Half a dozen times Denatti was forced to leap over the table to escape. The table was wide, and even in the frenzy of fear that had seized him, lending him unusual strength and agility, he was compelled to rest a hand upon the top in order to get over, while Fallon leaped clearly.

REVELLA had got to his feet, and with the sword in hand he now went to Denatti's aid. The two stood side by side, Denatti with the knife and Revella with the sword, and Fallon was forced to halt. He stood before them, crouching, seeking a point of attack, following Revella's sword point as it weaved and circled.

They could not use their weapons upon Fallon, for Fallon was quicker than the movement of Denatti's arm, and the point of the sword did not touch him. Yet Fallon could not stand or charge, for now while Revella forced him from the front, Denatti was attempting to slip around him to attack him from the rear. Fallon had to prevent that, and so he began to back away, circling around, keeping out of the corners.

It seemed that the two men were afraid of him. If both would attack, simultaneously, they would be almost certain of victory. But they did not. They followed him, always menacing him, backing him slowly around the room, attempting to crowd him into a corner. Meanwhile, being confident that sooner or later they would force him into a position from which there would be no escape, they taunted him. But Fallon, silent, grim, watchful, did not answer them.

Twice around the room they circled. The light held, but it was slowly going. The faces of the men were still visible to Fallon, and the light from the windows gleamed upon their weapons and upon the great sea chest at the west wall of the room, with its wide bands of brass.

A shaft of light reflected from some object outside the house, shone upon Denise, revealing her face with cameolike sharpness. The white light of the North, shimmering brightly and lasting long after the coming of darkness, created a subdued, pearly glow in the room.

Circling the room once more, Fallon suddenly leaped the table, leaving the two men in the open space toward the fireplace. Fallon reached for a heavy earthen jug in the center of the table.

Divining his purpose, Revella lunged at him with the sword. But Fallon, laughing derisively, gripped the jug, danced backward, then forward, and hurled the jug at Revella. It struck Revella in the chest. He staggered, coughed. His knees sagged. But he recovered quickly and came on again, cursing.

Revella moved west along the table, while Denatti went east. Fallon waited until they had rounded the ends and were coming toward him. Then he leaped over the table. As he went over, poised in mid-air, Denatti threw the knife. It whizzed past Fallon, missing his throat by inches, and struck the door through which Fallon had entered the room, sticking there, point first.

Fallon leaped for Denatti. But Denatti scurried out of his reach on the other side of the table, threw himself upon the knife that was sticking in the door, jerked it out and turned to face Fallon at the instant that Revella, following, came up.

Fallon had hurled himself at Denatti so swiftly that when the latter drew the knife from the door Fallon was forced to veer in his course to keep from crashing into the knife. He slid into the corner between the fireplace and the west door, and before he could turn, to leap again, Revella was upon him, forcing him back.

They had him now, in a corner.

SLOWLY they advanced upon him, Revella darting the sword in and out, Denatti with the long-bladed knife. He crouched low, meditating a rush upon Revella in which he might fend the inevitable sword-thrust with an arm, knock the man down, wrench the sword from his hand, and turn on Denatti.

Watching the men, weaving his body back and forth in an effort to induce Revella to lunge at him prematurely, Fallon perceived that the lid of the massive sea chest was rising. Rising with it were two brawny, reddish-brown arms, a head crowned with black hair, and mighty shoulders.

Wattanooka!

Fallon gave no sign that he had seen his friend. But the hard lines of his lips twitched into derisive curves as he continued to weave and sway his body in an effort to lure Revella into making a wild thrust. But the pair were sure of him now, and were closing slowly and carefully, making certain that this time he would not escape them.

Their backs were toward Wattanooka. The giant savage had stepped out of the chest and was advancing swiftly but cautiously. The huge belt-ax was in his right hand, its rawhide handle loop encircling his wrist. In the semi-darkness he appeared to be of monstrous size.

He stole upon the two men noiselessly. When he was within a step of Revella he stopped.

Denatti saw him. He straightened, stiffened, tried to cry out. But his voice caught in his throat and his eyes widened with horror. Fallon struck him then, a full, sweeping swing. The fist caught him on the point of the jaw and lifted him upward and backward. Into the shadows he crashed, his knife dropping to the floor at Fallon's feet.

There had been no sound from Revella, and no sword-thrust. Swiftly Fallon turned. Wattanooka had seized Revella from behind.

Revella was still facing Fallon. Wattanooka's right hand, the belt-ax dangling from the wrist, was clamped upon Revella's right arm, at the elbow. Revella's arm and the sword were sticking straight down so that the point of the weapon touched the floor. And the Indian's left arm was around Revella's neck. It was so big that it covered Revella's neck from chin to chest, and there was just enough pressure in its mighty muscles to hold Revella powerless to move.

Revella did not move. Out of the corners of his eyes he could see the big, reddish-brown arm, and he must have known now that what had happened to Mortwell and the two Crees was to happen to him.

FALLON had other things to think about than balking Wattanooka's meting out of justice—for the torturing Revella merited his fate.

Leaping to Denise's side, Fallon bent over her. She had not fainted, as he had thought, for her breath was coming regularly and slowly, as if in deep sleep. She had been drugged. Fallon's hand lingered on her forehead, as he flashed a glance toward the still motionless Denatti. Then, turning again, he saw Revella's face.

Wattanooka had wheeled Revella around so that now the

man faced him. The Indian's hands were gripping Revella's arms at the biceps. He had swung Revella from the floor and was holding him at arm's length. Revella's legs were dangling inertly; he was like a toy suspended from a string. His eyes were round with terror.

The sword had dropped from his nerveless fingers. He was looking straight into Wattanooka's eyes, and he knew that his doom was upon him. Under the spell of this scene, fascinated by the strangeness of the tragedy that was about to be enacted, Fallon stood motionless beside Denise, watching.

"Me Wattanooka," said the Indian.

Revella only stared.

"Ugh," grunted the Indian. "You know um, eh?"

A shudder ran over Revella.

"You Revella," continued Wattanooka. "You burn Adam Hammond with firebrand. You cut um with knife—make um talk. No talk—you kill um. You stick spear in Wattanooka. Come time—now. Break um neck."

Revella screamed.

Fallon moved to where Denatti had fallen. He bent over the man and found that he was dead. Whether from the blow or the fall, Fallon could not tell. And he had not time to waste with Denatti; for the front door burst open and one of the halberdiers leaped in.

He had heard Revella's scream.

The fellow saw what was happening to Revella, and he lunged forward, thrusting at Wattanooka with the sharp head of the halberd. The thrust was never completed, for again Fallon struck, leaping upon the halberdier from behind the half open door. The halberd clattered to the floor, and the man went down with it. He got up, staggering, and reached for a knife in his belt, under the foolish baldric. Fallon was measuring him for another blow when Wattanooka went past him like a giant shadow. The big belt-ax gleamed in the dying light.

The man's companion had entered the door, shoving his

awkward halberd ahead of him. The halberd caught crossways in the door. He lunged against it and rebounded. The belt-ax gleamed again.

Wattanooka kicked the halberd out of the way and closed the door. Both Wattanooka and Fallon, motionless for an instant following the fall of the second halberdier, observed a dozen canoes drawing up to the landing at the foot of the slope. In the canoes were white men. Two other white men were crossing the river.

The light was not strong, and yet it was reflected strongly enough from the water to permit Fallon to see the faces of the men. They were Kelso and Blandin. The other men, he decided, were the ruffians Randall had recruited for the raid upon Mercie Valley.

CHAPTER XXVIII

MADMAN'S CASTLE

WATTANOOKA CLOSED THE door. There was no word spoken. He restored the ax to his belt, stood erect and gazed about him with somber interest. The two halberdiers were lying between the big table and the front door. Over near the west wall, near where Fallon's pack had been, was Denatti. Revella, his head queerly twisted, was lying on his back in front of the fireplace.

Denatti's knife was lying on the floor near the west door, where he had dropped it when Fallon had hit him. Fallon had picked up the cartridges that Denatti had scattered, and was now testing and loading the weapon itself.

"Girl hurt?" asked Wattanooka.

"Drugged."

"What you mean?"

"Revella or Denatti give her big medicine. Bring sleep."

"Ugh." Wattanooka nodded his head toward the river: "White men come—strangers in canoe. Blandin. What do—fight um?"

"No. We'll get Denise away from here first."

"Good." He looked at Denise, stepped toward her, then looked at Fallon. "You carry," he added. "Come."

He went to the sea chest. It was now so dark that Fallon could not see his face, only the dim outline of his body, but he heard his short laugh.

"Box got no bottom. Wattanooka in tunnel. Find iron ladder. Come up. Now go down. Shut lid of box. No open from top."

Fallon descended, first passing Denise to Wattanooka. Then the Indian again ascended, fastened the lid of the chest and rejoined the two in the darkness below.

The passage they had entered ran at right angles from the main passage. Wattanooka lit a pine torch that he had brought with him when he had found the tunnel that led to the sea chest, and now he entered the main tunnel and lighted the way for Fallon.

They took Denise to her room and laid her upon her bed. She was still breathing slowly and regularly and gave no signs of returning consciousness. While Fallon was covering her with the quilts Wattanooka was at one of the windows, listening, and when Fallon finished with Denise he joined him.

"Cree down there," Wattanooka informed Fallon. "Many. Many white man. Blandin. They 'fraid. No go in house. What you do?"

"We'll try to find Underhill," said Fallon.

"Have to find pretty soon. Too many white men."

Fallon barred the door of Denise's room; then wrote a note to her telling her what had happened and advising her that if any danger threatened her from the hallway she should descend the shaft to the tunnel, where he and Wattanooka planned to continue their search for the missing Underhill. Then he and the Indian descended.

The big house was silent. Out in front where the Crees and the white men were congregated, there was whispering. The Crees were there out of curiosity, for they had watched the coming of the white men. But they were silent and nervous and they cast apprehensive glances toward the darkened windows of the house.

BLANDIN had been the first of the white men to reach the door, and Kelso was standing behind him when he knocked heavily upon it. Killen, Atkins and Eccles of the castle's regular residents, bringing the Crees from the village, had joined the men from the coast, telling Blandin what had happened.

Blandin, impotently raging, cursed Fallon. They had had to take Jackwoon back to Rossville, and had left Blanche Devake there.

When he learned that Lin Underhill had been secreted by Randall and could not be found, his rage was terrible to see.

He shoved the big inner door back so violently that the glass rattled. He stood for an instant in the doorway, confronted by a wall of blackness. A match flared in his hand and he held it above his head to peer into the room, with the white men behind him, and the Crees, overcoming their apprehensions, pressing against the doorway. They saw the two halberdiers, their heads split open by the belt-ax, lying in slowly spreading dark pools. They saw Denatti, lying flat on his back; they saw Revella's body, and his head, grotesquely twisted, the horrified eyes staring at them.

Some of the Crees had seen what the flickering blaze of the match had disclosed, and they fled, gibbering, to the foot of the slope. The match in Blandin's hand went out. And now came that breathless and shuddering pause which follows the discovery of tragedy grim and awful.

And in that instant, when the nerves of the men were tingling and jerking, there came a terrific clanking as of a sword sheath being hurled with frightful velocity down a flight of stone stairs; the sounds of furniture being tossed and tumbled about; the crashing and tinkling of broken glass; the banging of doors.

Above it all came a wild, high shriek of Gargantuan laughter, toneless and flat, carrying with it no mirth or joy of triumph, nor any sound that would express emotion of any kind. It came again immediately, changing its timbre so that in it could be detected a slight wailing. Again and again it came, filling the house, reverberating, echoing. Then the clanking came again, down the stairs, at the east door of the big room.

Blandin slammed the door shut, and followed the men, who had fled to the wharf.

"It's Randall," he muttered. "He's crazy as a loon!"

CHAPTER XXIX

A PIRATE'S SPORT

FOR A TIME, following Revella's departure, Randall had lain rigid. His hands had ceased beating the quilts, his legs had stopped jerking. His one eye stared fixedly at the ceiling. A complete paralysis seemed to have seized him. It had appeared to the doctor, Meeson, and to the others—even to Revella—that Randall was not aware of what was transpiring in his presence. That was because, having only one eye and no control of his facial muscles, his expression was blank.

But Randall's senses were alert. The blow that had broken his skull had affected his brain. Yet there were rays of light, flashes of consciousness and of reason. The fiery, whirling chaos wiped out much of the present and sent his mind skittering back into the happenings of the past.

He was again on the quarterdeck of the Terror, sailing the seven seas. Things were jumbled, puzzling. It was all right for him to see Meeson, the ship's doctor, but Denatti and Revella and Goodhull and the Jap had never been on his ship. And Denise—she had been on his ship, but only as a child. He couldn't get it straight. Denise shouldn't be here.

Meeson was talking about killing him with strychnine. Damn Meeson! He reached for his pistol, his cutlass. Not there.

Now Revella stood there, giving Denise something to drink—in a glass. Something that Meeson had given him. He tried to tell Denise not to drink it. He tried again to reach his pistol. Denise was limp in Revella's arms. Revella was carrying her away.

He strained; he fought to rise. Hours. Days.

He was up! Out of bed and staggering around the quarter-deck. His strength was back. He shrieked and yelled in glee. He hurled a boot through a mirror. Hell, the world had gone topsy-turvy! A bed on a quarterdeck. He hurled the table through a window, smashed the dresser on the stone floor.

He dressed, howling strange oaths, then took his heavy cutlass from a hook on the wall, and drew it out of the scabbard. He hurled the empty scabbard down the stairs, and with naked cutlass in hand followed it.

He lurched out into the big room. Dark. He found a match and lit the bracket lamp on the front wall, unaware that Blandin saw him, only to slam the door upon him. But he saw Denatti and Revella and the two halberdiers on the floor. He stood over the halberdiers and roared with Titanic laughter. All these dead men! They must have caught a merchantman. He did not re-member the fight. Dead and wounded. He called loudly for Meeson.

He raged, swinging his cutlass, when Meeson did not appear, and ran wildly up the stairs. At the far eastward end of the hall he saw Meeson emerging from his door. There was a candle in Meeson's hand and the light revealed Meeson's face, which was ghastly white. The candle fell from his hand, went out.

MEESON tried to flee from the house, but Randall almost caught him on the stairs. Meeson could hear the cutlass scrap-ing and clanging against the walls behind him.

He dove down the stairs as he felt the cutlass singing close to his head. He landed at the bottom with the breath knocked out of him, and lurched out into the big room, in the light from the bracket lamp. Meeson was hurt. He knew he could not get to the door in time, and so he stooped, picked up Revella's sword, and faced the madman.

Some of the bolder men from the coast, peering in through

the windows, saw him lunge at Randall with the sword; they saw the big cutlass shatter the slender blade to fragments that rang and clattered upon the floor. And they saw the cutlass flash in gleaming half circles as Meeson was cut down, falling at last near Revella.

Then Randall paused. He turned slowly around and stared at the windows. His solitary eye was gleaming with a fierce, wild light. His face was red, blotched with purple. The cords of his neck were bulged and knotty. He suddenly picked up an earthen jug from the table and hurled it with deadly aim at one of the windows, howling: "Back to your quarters, you hellions!"

He roared when the faces vanished. Then he turned back to roam through the house, giving orders to imaginary men. He called the members of his old crew by name. He was again at sea, and the house was his ship. He captured a prize, transferred her stores to his own vessel, and sank her. He ordered the crew of the captured ship put to death, and he laughed and roared as two men were forced to walk the plank. Then, suddenly, he thought of Denise.

He tried her door and found it locked from the inside. He begged for admittance, promising that if she would open the door he would tell her something. When he was not admitted he began to pound on the door with the hilt of the cutlass; and when that failed he began to rage again. Entering a near-by room, he lifted the hearthstone from the fireplace and hurled the stone out of a window, yelling with glee at the crashing of the glass. He went down into it to the tunnel, to enter the room adjoining Denise's.

The door entering Denise's room was open, and he strode to the girl's bed and stood looking down at her. Sight of her seemed to calm him a little, and he talked to her, apparently not understanding that he received no answers.

He left her bedside and stood beside the shaft in the other room, staring into it. And as he stared his eyes gleamed slyly. He laughed, went down the shaft, and began to walk through the main tunnel.

CHAPTER XXX

UNDERGROUND

FALLON AND WATTANOOKA had separated. The Indian, in his secret prowling about the house—into Mowaki's kitchen and the store room, and even into the outbuildings at the rear—had found a short, heavy iron bar with a flat, sharp end; and with this, as Fallon left him, he began to prod and poke at the stones that lined the main tunnel. He had persistently insisted that Underhill would be found in one of the passages under the house, and he worked patiently to vindicate his judgment.

Fallon had gone outside, letting himself into the open through the river entrance to the passage. He was of the opinion that Randall had secreted Underhill somewhere in the timber, fearing that Denatti or Revella or the others might find him in the house.

Wattanooka, working in the main passage, had several times paused to listen to faint, strange noises that came from the floors above him. At last he moved along the passage until he reached the small tunnel that led to the shaft under the sea chest. Climbing the ladder, he placed his head against the under side of the lid of the chest and listened.

Plainly he could hear Randall raging and raving. He heard the clang of metal, the crashing of glass. But he shrank when he finally realized that Randall was insane, for the superstitions of his race told him that a crazy man was one who was inspired and actuated by evil spirits. He wanted nothing to do with

Randall, so he silently descended to the tunnel and resumed his work upon the walls.

He was working in the light of a pine torch that he had stuck in a crack in the rock floor; but suddenly he leaped upon the torch and stamped out the blaze, for he had heard some one coming down a distant shaft. He seized the torch, which was still smoking, and ran into an intersecting tunnel to hide until he learned the identity of the intruder. It might be Denise, though she had been sleeping soundly. It could not be Fallon, who was outside in the woods. It might be Randall, for Randall knew of the passages, having built them.

It was Randall.

He was entering the passage from the shaft that led to the room next to Denise's, and Wattanooka drew the ax from his belt. Superstition was strong in him, but he decided that if Randall was carrying Denise from her room he would kill him. For he knew that Fallon loved Denise.

Randall had a pine torch. He had taken it from a niche in the wall of the tunnel. He had them hidden everywhere. He dropped heavily into the passage and stood under the shaft for a time, peering about. The rays from the torch penetrated the darkness for only a short distance, but Randall appeared to be satisfied, for he finally went eastward, the torch held in front of him.

He was muttering. He stopped at every shaft and peered into it. He examined the entrance to every cross tunnel. Watching him intently, Wattanooka decided that his malady had passed the violent stage. A little less apprehensive, Wattanooka followed.

He kept out of the radius of the light rays and took advantage of every cross tunnel he came to, but Randall did not look back.

He paused at last far down the passage, and ran his torch along the rock wall as if searching for something. Then he placed a hand against the wall and leaned his weight against it. The hand disappeared to the elbow, and beside it a rectangular section about four or five feet square swung slowly outward into the tunnel.

WATTANOOKA stared in amazement. The section was on hinges. The rocks that formed the wall were on a background of steel or iron, and were so cleverly fitted and matched that the outline of the door could not be detected except by a minute examination. Wattanooka was certain he had many times inspected that very section of the wall.

Randall shoved the door back against the wall, and propped it open with a rock that he picked up from the dark interior beyond the open door. He was so careful about placing the rock in position that Wattanooka got the impression that the door could not be opened from the inside, and that Randall was making certain it would not accidentally close and imprison him.

Randall finally seemed satisfied. He stepped into the doorway, torch in hand. Wattanooka could hear his boot heels clattering on the rock floor. Wattanooka leaped to the doorway and peered after Randall. The latter was walking slowly, swaying from side to side, like a bear. The torch he carried gleamed and flickered upon the ragged rock walls and ceiling of this unknown passage that broadened like a wedge, the doorway being the narrowest point.

This evidently was a sort of store room. Boxes, bales and barrels were strewn along the walls. There was a row of shelving, laden with small, fat canvas bags—bags of gunpowder. There were hundreds of them.

Randall did not appear to be interested in the stores. He opened a door that was cut into the wall at his left, pushed it back so that it would not close, and stepped into the opening. It was several seconds before Wattanooka ventured to approach the doorway, and when he did so he again saw Randall.

The man was standing near the center of a big cavern which was flooded with light that entered through iron bars that covered an opening to the outside world. Willows, growing outside the bars, screened the entrance, and a shadow entering with the light indicated a rock wall or a hill close to the willows. There was a door in the entrance, chained and locked.

Randall had dropped the torch, for there was no need of its light here. Randall stood with his back to Wattanooka, and directly in front of Randall, sitting upon a stool, his wrists in irons which were attached to the wall behind him by chains, was a young man instantly recognized by Wattanooka as Lin Underhill.

In Wattanooka's eyes Underhill had changed very little. He seemed to have lost no weight during his confinement, though his face bore a pallor that had replaced the healthy tan that Wattanooka knew. He was tall, lithe, with broad shoulders that sloped like an athlete's. His black hair was in disorder and dropped in long waves over his ears and the back of his neck; and a six months' growth of beard added to the wildness of his appearance. Yet Wattanooka knew him.

He did not see Wattanooka. He was watching Randall, steadily, inquiringly, fearlessly, and Wattanooka saw his muscles begin to tense as Randall reached into a pocket and drew out a key.

Randall swayed back and forth like a bear standing on its hind legs. The key, which was small, dangled between the thumb and forefinger of his right hand. Wattanooka could not see his face, but he intently watched Randall, and he saw the young man's eyes begin to gleam with amazement and furtive hope. It appeared to Wattanooka that Underhill understood what had happened to Randall.

And now Randall spoke. His voice was hoarse and quavering with passion.

"You won't tell, eh?" he said. "You won't tell where Hammond's gold is hid? You claim you don't know anything about it. Hammond told you. But you say he didn't. You lying lubber! The gold is hid somewhere in the hold of this ship. You told Revella where to find it and he tried to get it without letting me know. But I caught him. I caught him on the quarterdeck and cut his throat. And that's what I'm going to do with you, my hearty."

He dropped the key—he seemed to have forgotten it—and drew a knife. He had placed the cutlass on Denise's bed when he had been talking to her in her room, and in his wanderings about the house he had picked up the long knife that Denatti had dropped when Fallon had hit him.

UNDERHILL leaped to his feet as Randall, crouching and muttering, moved toward him.

Wattanooka's rush was swift and noiseless.

Randall was within a few feet of Underhill when the giant savage gripped him from behind. Swiftly a big, reddish-brown arm slipped around Randall's neck, constricting with resistless force until the man's breath was shut off and his popping eye stared at the ceiling. Wattanooka's right arm went over Randall's shoulder, holding it tightly against his side, while the big hand slipped down and grasped the wrist of Randall's hand holding the knife.

There followed the strange rasping sound of the bodies of two strong men clenched in combat; the furious and breathless straining of strength pitted against strength, when muscles are tried to their utmost. Randall was a huge man, and heavy, but his feet slowly left the rock floor as his body was bent backward. The knife clanged, dropping from Randall's hand and sliding across the floor to the bars of the entrance, where it lay, gleaming in the light.

Randall threshed, fought to turn, but the iron arms that held him were rigid and unyielding. And yet, heaving mightily, with all the fury and strength that his malady gave him, he gained an inch. Wattanooka's arm slipped along his great, bull-like neck. It stopped at the chin and Randall's body grew limp. Still the Indian's arm held him. A minute, perhaps. Then the grip relaxed. Randall slumped to the floor. His face was mottled, the brutal lips were blue.

Wattanooka found the key that Randall had dropped, leaped to Underhill and unlocked the manacles. The chains rattled against the rock wall, and Wattanooka and Underhill went through the open doorway into the store room.

In the store room they paused to grip hands, then went swiftly through the wedge-like passage to the main tunnel. Here Wattanooka found his pine torch, lighted it and closed the iron door to the tunnel.

"Shut him in," he said, thinking of Randall. "No kill um. Crazy."

He led Underhill through the main tunnel to the entrance at the edge of the river. There they found Fallon's pack. They climbed out of the entrance and for a few minutes they stood there while Underhill gratefully drank the keen, fresh air of the open.

"No hurry," Wattanooka informed him. "You weak. Hungry. No get grub for long time. Huh?"

"I had plenty of food and water," answered Underhill. "They were brought to me by a Cree from the village. It was always the same one. I think he was the only one of the Indians who knew where Randall had taken me. I haven't suffered much. At first they were pretty rough with me. But that's nothing. Is Gail all right?"

"Gail well. Worry about you. Send Wattanooka and Fallon to find you."

"Fallon! Who is Fallon?"

"Big man. White man. Strong. Brave. You father send um to north country."

Wattanooka would say no more until they had traveled some miles southward, to the shelter that he and Fallon had prepared. There, stretched out on the bed of yielding branches that were like down to Underhill, Wattanooka related the story of Fallon's pilgrimage into the land.

"Where is Fallon now?" asked Underhill. "I would like to thank him."

"Ugh," grunted the Indian. "Him come bimeby. Think um bring woman."

CHAPTER XXXI

BLANDIN EXPLORES

THE SCENE THAT Blandin and the other white men had witnessed when they had stared through the windows of the big room had shaken their courage. Eccles and his companions were accustomed to bloodshed, but the tableau in that room, and then the spectacle of the giant madman cutting Meeson to pieces had been too much for them and they fled down the river toward the Indian village, the coast men with them. The Indians had preceded them.

The white men were standing apart from the Indians. The coast men were silent, listening to Eccles, who told them what had happened. A shudder ran through them when Eccles related how men had been found with their necks broken. The Crees were in a panic and could not be induced to go to Mercie Valley. They wanted nothing to do with "The Neckbreaker," who had grown tall as a tree in their superstitious stories. Eccles and his two friends, Killen and Atkins, and the Japanese, Mowaki, stole to the landing, embarked in canoes and started down the river toward the coast, while the Crees broke camp.

Blandin, who had been silent, watched them go. The men from the coast sullenly stood their ground, but they posted sentries when they made camp.

Blandin had his own opinion about what had happened. He knew Wattanooka and he knew Fallon, and he surmised that the two had met and had come to the stone house to search for Underhill. The Indian legends about Wattanooka were legends only. Wattanooka was a big man, to be sure, but he was not supernatural and a bullet would bring him down as quickly as it would bring down an ordinary man. As for Fallon, a bullet, rightly placed, would finish him also. And Blandin was eager to speed such a bullet, for he still remembered the terrible beating he had received that night on the steamer.

Also, there was rioting in Blandin's veins a lust for the gold in Mercie Valley, and there burned in him the hot desire of a man for a woman. He had seen Denise several times and her disdainful manner toward him had merely inflamed him the more. He was not sure that Underhill had starved to death. There was a chance that Randall—crazy as he was—would recover. Denise was still in the house, for during the excitement he had questioned Eccles about her.

So he had stood quietly with the other men, listening, feeling a deep contempt for their cowardice, never for an instant sharing their fears or harboring a furtive impulse toward panic.

TOWARD morning Randall's voice was heard no more, and presently Blandin began to steal up the slope toward the house. He opened the front door, stepped inside, and listened. He heard no sound and was now convinced that Randall's ragings had exhausted him; the weakness due to his injury had reasserted itself.

He stood for a time looking at the dead men that were strewn all over the room, and then he crossed the big room and went up the stairway to Randall's room.

The first gray streaks of dawn were coming in the windows, and he was able to see that Randall was not in his bed. He smiled wryly at the wreck of the room, stepped back into the hallway and went down it, trying doors that were closed and peering into rooms whose doors were open and finding them empty.

Daylight had come by the time he got downstairs again, and when he reached the big room he blew out the bracket lamp. His rage was deep, for his plans had gone awry, but his lust and greed were great and he entertained no thought of defeat. When he met Fallon again he would square things with him. If he could find Randall he would tie him up against the time when his malady would permit him to talk rationally, then he would find Underhill and torture the truth out of him. And even if he did not find Underhill, he would kill Wattanooka, recruit Crees, go to Mercie Valley and find the gold. He would seize the big house; and Denise would stay there with him.

Such were his thoughts as he climbed the west stairway and went along the hall. He knew which was Denise's room. He placed an ear against the door, and could hear her breathing. He smiled and stealthily tried the door. Then he stepped into another room, where he had observed that the hearthstone was missing. He suspected that perhaps through it he might solve the riddle of the mysterious movements of Wattanooka in the house, as told him by Eccles.

It was now broad day, and when Blandin stood over the mouth of the shaft under the fireplace he could see the iron rungs of the ladder. He laughed gleefully and went down the shaft, to drop lightly to the stone floor of the tunnel.

He found a pine torch that some one had dropped, and he lit it and stood there holding it above his head while he gazed about him. He wasn't greatly interested in the system of passages, though it was clever of Randall to conceive them. He had no doubt that Randall was down here—sleeping off his exhaustion probably—and that Underhill would be found here.

There was time. He was alone. None of the white men would enter the house, and the Crees were moving northward.

Lighting his way with the torch, he saw the various shafts. He climbed one or two, shoving the hearthstones aside and looking into the rooms. And then he climbed one where the hearthstone had already been removed, and he rested in the opening, listening to the breathing of some one in the room adjoining. He smiled, swung himself out of the shaft, and cautiously stepped to the communicating door. He saw Denise lying on the bed where Fallon had placed her.

CHAPTER XXXII

BATTLE OF TITANS

DAY HAD COME when Fallon returned to the mouth of the tunnel, after having spent the night prowling about the country. He slipped into the entrance, closed it, and lit a pine torch from a supply that Wattanooka had found. He was beginning to believe that Underhill would never be found—that Randall had killed him.

He had no thought of giving up; but must take Denise to where she would be safe from the band of murderers that inhabited the house, and from Blandin and the other white men he had seen at the landing. He could take her to Mercie Valley, but he would have to accompany her on the trip, and during his absence he would have to give up his search for Underhill. He was certain she would not agree to go there with Wattanooka, for the Indian was a stranger and she was afraid of him.

While he walked from the entrance to the shaft that led to the room next to Denise's he decided. He would take Denise from the house. If she was still under the influence of the drug, that had been given her, he would carry her to the shelter Wattanooka had built, wait there with her until she recovered, and then take her to Mercie Valley. Wattanooka could stay near the stone house and continue the search for Underhill. He could make the trip to the valley and back in seven or eight days.

He climbed the shaft, stepped out of it and moved lightly to the door that opened into Denise's room. He saw Blandin standing at the bedside, looking down at Denise, who had regained consciousness and was staring up at the intruder with startled, incredulous fright and horror. She seemed to lack the power to move or cry out, for she was motionless and no sound came from her open lips.

Blandin's back was toward Fallon. And Fallon stood silent, watching. Blandin's revolver was in his right hand. He tossed it upon the bed, where it dropped beside Randall's cutlass. Randall had laid the weapon there when he had been insanely talking to the girl. And now Blandin laughed, and bent over Denise to speak to her. He must have seen something in the girl's eyes that warned him of a presence behind him, for he turned swiftly, saw Fallon, and lunged for the gun or the cutlass—one or the other.

He got neither. There was no time. For he had to turn to meet Fallon's rush, to dodge the terrific blow that started for him with all the force of Fallon's rage behind it. The fist grazed the top of his head as he evaded it, but he was not prepared for the sudden impact of Fallon's weight, and both men went down in a threshing tangle, over in a corner near a window, into a wreck of furniture that crashed and clattered around them.

Appalled, shocked out of the coma into which the drug had sent her, but still breathless and speechless, Denise sat up and stared at the raging men. They rolled over and over, taking the furniture with them. They rose and fought near the wreck of Denise's dressing table, and Blandin toppled over it to land upon his shoulders with his heavy, muscular legs sticking straight into the air. He seemed impervious to injury. His bulging thighs and arms and shoulders were sheathed with flesh that seemed like rubber, for he rebounded from falls that might have broken the bones of an ordinary man, and plunged into Fallon with the fury of a beast deprived of its kill.

Fallon also appeared not to feel the bumps and blows. The furniture might have been made of *papier-mâché*. It cracked and crashed under their weight and was threshed and churned under their rolling bodies until the room seemed to be filled with débris.

THE SOUNDS went through an open window of the room and carried to the Indian village, where they were heard by the white men who were camped there. The men ran to the foot of the slope near the landing and stood there listening, although they could see nothing. They thought, perhaps, that the noise was made by Randall, in his madman's antics; and they did not approach the house, but stood there, silent and awed.

Fallon might have drawn the gun whose stock stuck out of the holster at his side. He did not think of it. The cold fury that seethed in him was concentrated in an effort to beat and maim the hated face that ducked and dodged in front of him, and at times was laid on his shoulder as they wrestled here and there, striving, straining for advantage.

Blandin, broad, shorter than Fallon, was astonishingly light on his feet; and somewhere, doubtless in other fights in which he had engaged, he had learned the art of slipping and ducking blows.

For he was as elusive as a shadow, and Fallon had trouble hitting him. Not once so far had Fallon been able to land a solid punch, although he had started many. They had glanced off Blandin's head and chin, or had gone around Blandin's neck as he stepped forward. In the clinches Blandin would brace his stocky legs, rest his head against Fallon's chest and shove forward, driving terrific blows with both hands.

There was no word spoken. Crouching on the bed Denise watched the set faces and the blazing eyes of the two men and knew that this was to be a battle that would not end until one of the fighters was dead. She winced as Blandin drove in blows that would have shivered a plank, but when she saw that they had no apparent effect upon Fallon she felt a fierce, wild exultation.

For five, ten, fifteen minutes they fought, seemingly upon even terms, though Blandin had landed the greater number of blows. But now Denise sensed a change. Blandin was fighting as furiously as ever, and it seemed there would be no end to his terrific energy, no wearing of the tough muscles that propelled him here and there with a rapidity that baffled Fallon.

It was Fallon who had brought about the change. At first his rage had made him too eager. Now he had control of himself. He was measuring his blows; he was coldly calculating distance. Twice his fists had reached Blandin's head with the vicious snap and jar that told of perfect timing, and Blandin's knees sagged.

Again, lunging forward with his head down, Blandin ran into an upper-cut that snapped his head back and sent him reeling to the wall. Fallon was after him swiftly. Blandin was badly hurt, but he roared with rage, bounced forward with his head down and drove himself like a battering ram into Fallon's stomach.

Fallon staggered. His face turned ashen. His legs doubled under him; he went to one knee and his chin sank to his chest as Blandin launched a furious kick at him. Blandin was too eager. The boot went over Fallon's head, and he was up, gripping Blandin around the waist in an effort to hang on until the pain left him. Blandin, fighting now with demoniac fury, fought to shake Fallon off, and again they careened around the room in the débris.

Blandin shook himself loose, stepped back and came in again, to be met with a terrific punch that stopped him in his tracks. He came on again, blinking, trying to shake off the mental fog that had suddenly enveloped him, striving to get close so that he could clinch with Fallon.

THE MEN had forgotten Denise; they did not even glance at her; it seemed they were oblivious of their surroundings, to the room, to the wreck and ruin they had wrought, to the débris through which they plunged in their efforts to beat and maim each other.

Blandin had become a beast; he had reverted to type; his was an atavism. Cornered in this room, with a man he knew was his equal if not his superior, given no chance to get at the gun he had carelessly thrown upon the bed, forced to fight with only the weapons that nature had given him, he was a brute in the last extremity, and he muttered and whined and mewed insanely as he drove forward, swinging his fists.

Locked together, they swayed around the room. They went down in a corner and rolled over and over to the center, to rise and separate as though by prearrangement, to meet again with a crash as Fallon's fist met Blandin's jaw.

Blandin went down, but was up again instantly. Blood was streaming down his face. His lips were macerated, there were big, purple bruises on his cheeks; his nose was awry—broken, it seemed. But still he kept coming, getting up from the floor after each knockdown and launching himself like a projectile at his enemy. Fallon's blows, accurately placed, driven with appalling force, had no apparent effect upon him. He shook his head as if to clear his brain, and came in again.

Denise was on her knees on the bed, breathlessly watching, her body swaying as her tensed nerves reacted sympathetically to Fallon's movements. At first she had anticipated an easy victory for Fallon, but as the fight went on and she saw that his blows had little effect upon Blandin she began to fear that Blandin would win.

She had knelt there, clasping her hands, desperately and frenziedly twining and untwining her fingers. But now, realizing that perhaps Fallon would not win, she got the gun that Blandin had tossed upon the bed, cocked if and held it with both hands and waited. If Blandin won and stood free, she would shoot him.

Outside, creeping slowly up the slope, crowding closer, spurred by curiosity to learn the identity of the fighters in the room, the coast men several times saw Blandin and Fallon as they fought close to the windows.

One window was wide open and through it went the sound of the wrecked furniture being kicked out of the way by the raging men; through the window went Blandin's voice as he whined and cursed and muttered. The men saw Blandin's face, smashed, but still recognizable to those who knew him; they saw Fallon's face, grim, cold, determined. And now, knowing that it was not the crazy Randall who was creating the din, some of the men darted toward the front door.

Denise had not seen them enter the house, but she heard them in the hallway.

Knowing nothing of the secret entrance or of the tunnels under the house, the men were at the doors, trying to open them, but not succeeding because of the heavy fastenings. The men who had stayed outside had crowded still closer. They were shouting encouragement to Blandin. They dared not shoot at that swift flurry of bodies.

However, they could not help Blandin. The fight was almost over. Twice, coldly measuring the distance, Fallon had knocked Blandin down. It was the beginning of the end.

Blandin was staggering. His bull-like strength was deserting him and his recuperative power was on the wane. Getting up from the second knockdown he stood for an instant swaying, his eyes blinking. But he surged forward again, into a swishing fist that struck his jaw with a sound like that of an ax splitting a log. His legs bent at the knees, his body twisted so that he bent forward from the hips. He went to his hands and knees and rested there, swaying from side to side. Then he got up, slowly, and backed away from Fallon.

He knew the end had come. It seemed he was mutely signalling surrender. Then suddenly he leaped for the cutlass on the bed. His right hand was within an inch of the handle when Fallon, stirred to a sudden, furious rage, struck him again. Blandin went down without a sound, and this time he did not rise to renew the battle.

For a moment Fallon stood, watching him, listening. He heard the coast men at the door; he could hear the others outside the house. He stooped over Blandin, seized him by the shoulder and a leg and swung him slowly over his head. Then, with a mighty tensing of body muscles, he threw Blandin out of the open window, and watched him land on his head in the midst of the coast men. Then he turned to Denise.

She sprang to meet him, knowing the danger of delaying. They went down the shaft in the next room, through the main tunnel to the entrance, crossed the river at the point where the Cree had hurled the spear at Fallon, and entered the dark forest that began at the water's edge. There Fallon found a game trail that he and Wattanooka had used.

Denise was trembling. He faced her, drew her to him and held her tightly, protectively, for a moment. Then, lifting her to his shoulder, he ran southward, toward the shelter that Wattanooka had built.

CHAPTER XXXIII

RANDALL'S LAST JEST

A FEW MINUTES after Wattanooka and Lin Underhill left the cavern Randall began to twist and squirm. Slowly the dark color stole from his face, to be succeeded by an ashen paleness. Still unconscious, he clawed at his neck, where the Indian's great arm had been. He rolled his head from side to side, fighting his way back to life, for he had been near death.

He was not aware of his narrow escape, and when at last he opened his eye and stared at the ceiling of the cavern he had no recollection of what had happened to him. In his imagination he was still on the deck of his ship, and when he finally sat up, gasping for breath he was trying to shout orders to his crew.

But that phase passed, and at about the time Blandin was going through the tunnel in search of a shaft that would lead him to Denise's room, Randall was standing before the powder shelves in the store room slyly cackling. He was now in the hold of the ship. What had he gone into the hold for? To sink the ship, of course—to blow it up. A brig of war—a British ship of the line—had crippled him, was about to board. His crew were dead or wounded.

The Englishman wanted to capture him, to take him to England in irons, then to hang him. Damned if he'd surrender. They'd all go down together! There was the powder right in front of him. Powder and fuses. Tons of powder, miles of fuses.

He filled his arms with sacks of the powder and coils of fuses and ran to the door that opened into the main passage. Wattanooka had thought the door could not be opened from the inside, but Randall fumbled at it an instant and swung it ajar. He propped it open and ran down the main tunnel to one that intersected. He stayed in it for a time, packing the bags of powder away.

He ran back to the store room after more bags of the explosive, and when he was satisfied with what he had done he ran a fuse into the intersecting tunnel and stretched it down the main tunnel. He ran here and there into other intersecting tunnels, carrying bags of powder, arranging them and stringing fuses.

He seemed to have a comprehensive plan. Perhaps in the sane months and years before insanity came he had planned this act, rehearsing it over and over mentally until he had it complete, until every detail had been thought out. But whether or not he had previously planned it, there was no hesitation in his manner.

When he had stowed more than half the bags in the tunnels he climbed the shaft that led to the sea chest in the big room and placed a number of bags in the various rooms, running a separate system of fuses to the sea chest. He packed the powder with earth and stone, in closets and in secret apertures, until he had it scattered all over the house, above and below.

Several times he heard sounds that brought him to a pause to listen. A rending and a crashing upstairs; voices outside. He peered out of a window and saw the coast men congregated at the bottom of the slope. They were all staring up and their faces were set. He saw a body hurtle down, to strike the granite of the slope headforemost, and he laughed in high glee at the spectacle.

He saw some of the men running toward the front door, and he dived headlong into the sea chest and then popped his head out under the lowered lid to watch them as they charged through the big room to reach the upper floor. Not one of them had seen the fuses that were cunningly strung along the floor in the corners.

HE HOWLED as he applied a match to the fuses, and when they fizzed and sputtered, and the white, acrid smoke began to run along the floor, following the white, sizzling sparks that ran along the various fuse lines, he bellowed hilariously, clambered down the ladder under the sea chest and ran to the store room.

There, bending over the ends of the fuses he had laid in the subterranean passages, lighted match in hand, he heard the dull boom of an explosion upstairs. The air around him rocked; the rumble shook the rock floor under him. Then came another explosion, and another. There was a crash on the floor above him, and a roar just above his head.

He danced up and down, yelling delightedly.

The match he was holding went out. He lit another and bent again to light the fuses at his feet. They caught. Fiery serpents crawled and wriggled away from him. They went out of the door of the store room and into the main tunnel. Some of them went east, others went west.

He leaned against the door jambs and laughed until he began to choke. He heard a terrific bombing all around him—like thunder above his head. There was a continual crashing, as of beams falling. These sounds seemed far away and muffled.

He waited, and at last there was a detonation in the tunnel that caught him, lifted him and hurled him far back into the store room. It threw him flat and he tried to rise, to howl the glee that sought expression. He was hurled back again as another blast smote him.

The rock walls around him began to split asunder. Through a bluish white smoke that swirled and eddied around him, he saw great crevices in the walls and ceilings. The shelves in the store room toppled over and fell upon him.

He kicked them out of the way and tried to get up. But

something was wrong with him. He could not rise. What was it?

He saw the ceiling above him part and crumble. Great blocks of rock slipped down and struck near him with a terrific thudding sound. The big end of the cavern collapsed, the walls slipped inward, toward him.

CHAPTER XXXIV

HEADED OUTSIDE

DENISE AND FALLON had reached Wattanooka's shelter
and had met the rescued Underhill when the sound of the first
booming explosion reached them, and they had listened until
the last one came and the quivering air again became heavy
with its brooding silence.

Fallon and Wattanooka went back to the edge of the forest.
The great house had fallen. It was now only a flattened pile of
stone and beams, bearing no resemblance to anything that man
has constructed. Here and there upon the pile of débris were
the torn and mangled bodies of men. A faint, blue smoke spi-
ralled here and there from the rocks.

The Cree village was deserted. Lashed to the little landing
at the foot of the granite slope were many canoes, empty. The
binnacle had been overthrown. It had slid to the bottom of the
slope and its polished brass glittered in the sunlight.

Already the primeval wilderness was reverting to the somber
silence which had reigned over it until Lumly Randall and his
band had broken it. For now there were no sounds from the
house. Lumly Randall had come to disturb the peace of this
solitude, and now peace had again returned. Only the twitter-
ing of birds and the slow, steady sweep of a gently sighing breeze
from the south broke the somber silence.

At the shelter Denise listened, dry-eyed, to the description
of the ruin that had overtaken the stone house. She slipped into

Fallon's arms and stood, holding him tightly. And at this minute Fallon said nothing to her.

They spent a week in Mercie Valley, and were on their way down the river going toward the secret entrance through which Fallon had first penetrated the Hammond domain, when Denise spoke a thought that had been troubling her.

Wattanooka had insisted upon accompanying them to Rossville. Lin Underhill was not going out for another month, but Fallon was bearing a message to the elder Underhill, which would be telegraphed from Grand Marias. In the party with Denise and Fallon were Wattanooka and another Indian, to carry the luggage and to make the camps.

They were traveling slowly, and the wilderness was smiling under a summer sun. The long stretches of smooth water in the rivers and lakes made a gently undulating pathway for their canoes, and the green of the forests provided their beds for the nights.

Fallon's canoe was foremost. He wielded the paddle, and during the daylight hours Denise sat facing him, watching him. Wattanooka and the other Indian were always several hundred yards behind.

Denise was watching the water as it rippled in graceful swells away from the bow of the canoe. She was blushing, but her eyes were serene under their drooping lids.

"Ah, Monsieur Jim," she almost whispered, "you are a very determined man. You know that Lumly Randall died without revealing my identity. Yet you would marry me—a nameless girl."

"I am not going to marry a name. I want you yourself, dear, name or no name."

Silence came. Denise broke it, saying:

"Jim, do you remember that day in my room in the stone house when you leaned over me when I was sitting in the chair?"

"I remember every second I have passed with you."

"And do you remember what you said then?"

"Yes."

"Will you say it again?"

"A thousand times. It was: 'Denise, you are my woman.'"

"It is the same," she smiled.

There was silence again, and the canoe entered a patch of shade, where the surface of the water was like a mirror with a shadow upon it.

And then Denise looked at Fallon steadily.

"Jim," she said. "I'm sorry. I mocked you that day, and while I was mocking you I wanted to cry. I did not want to love you until I knew there could never be any doubt in your mind that you loved me. Yet if you had asked me I should have answered that you are my man. Jim, I knew it from the first time I saw you."

The canoe lingered in the patch of shade. Far down the river Wattanooka observed that the leading canoe was motionless, idly drifting with the lazy current; so he headed the prow of his own craft into some willows that fringed the bank, and motioned to the other Indian to join him.

ABOUT THE AUTHOR

THE VITAL STATISTICS are: Born in August, 1875, at the village of Janesville, Wisconsin. One year in Wisconsin. Then to Columbus, Ohio, where the educational process was begun, and where after a time I worked at various enterprises, such as newsboy, telegraph messenger, painter, carpenter and manager of the circulation of a newspaper. Spent the better part of five summers and some of the winters in Union County, New Mexico. At twenty I was in Cleveland, Ohio, where I was again a carpenter. Foreman, contractor. Began to write about this time—nights. Thirteen years of writing without finding a publisher. In the interim I was engaged in various enterprises: Building inspector for the City of Cleveland, editor of a small newspaper, expert for the Cuyahoga County Board of Appraisers. Wrote and sold about one hundred short stories. Published a book of short stories called the *Range Riders* in 1911. A success. Followed it with a full length novel called *The Two-Gun Man* in 1911. Another bell-ringer. *Gone North* will be the thirtieth published book. Twenty-three of these have been published as serials in *Argosy*.

I have no regular working hours, but I try my best to turn out at least two full length serials each year. I still make an occasional trip to the West. I like to go over the old ranges. I do not like to have any one refer to Western stories as "wild and woolly," because, while I concede that the West was wild, it never became woolly until the advent of the sheep—and that was after I lived there. I never saw a pair of sheep chaps; I never

heard a cowhand call another "cowboy,"
"cow-puncher" or "waddie." "Hand," or
"rider," or "cowhand" was the radius of
the terminology as applied to the
regular ranch employee. "Straw-boss,"
"wrangler," "buster," "range-boss" were
others—all understandable and uni-
versal in the Southwest. To be sure,
there were Mexican equivalents used.

*Charles Alden
Seltzer*

I have made some trips into the
country which I have written about in
Gone North. Fishing, hunting and ob-
serving. My hobbies are hunting, fishing, trap shooting, pistol
practice and politics. I have broken ninety-two out of a possible hundred clay targets. In a pistol shoot in competition—
with a thirty-eight Colt—at twenty yards I have made a
ninety-one and a quarter per cent target.

Last November I rang the bell in North Olmsted politics by
being elected mayor of the town—and I am now serving my
sentence. North Olmsted is a suburban town on the edge of
Cleveland and has a population of twenty-five hundred people
and by the end of my two-year term I expect they will all join
in chasing me out of town.

I have been married thirty-five years. Five children. One girl
married, one at home. One boy, Louis B., is editor of the Cleveland *Press;* another, Robert M., is a star reporter; the third is
an advertising man. I am grateful that they did not attempt to
follow in their father's footsteps.

P.S. My wife still believes in me.

ABOUT THE ARTIST

PAUL STAHR, WHO painted this week's cover and many other outstanding *Argosy* cover illustrations, is a New Yorker born and bred. He attended school in Yorkville, at P.S. 86 and Morris High School. From the very beginning he turned to art as his life-work, studying at the Academy and the Art Students' League, where he had the benefit of instruction by George Bridgman.

Stahr was one of the pioneers in the art colony on Washington Heights, which has probably replaced Greenwich Village as the actual, if not the traditional, center of New York's palette-wielders.

Like all budding artists, Stahr had to do considerable hack work at the start; and he chose the theatrical field, painting posters for new shows. If the Shuberts or Savage or some other big producer of those days opened a new show, Stahr would be sent on a moment's notice to the city where the play was being "tried out on the dog," to sketch some of the people and scenes of the drama. Then would come the hectic business of getting the posters made from his drawings or paintings in time for the Broadway opening. More than once he had to do his sketches on the train as he was rushing back to New York—no mean feat, as any one can testify who has tried the comparatively simple task of writing a letter on the train.

This early poster work, of which artists are never very fond, was turned to fine patriotic account by Stahr in war days, when he did many of the most successful posters for the Hoover Food Administration, the Red Cross, the Liberty Loans, and the various branches of national defense. This work, contributed gratis by Stahr and his fellow artists, was an important factor in keeping up the country's morale during those troublous times.

Besides Stahr's vivid and interesting cover paintings for *Argosy,* he has done a good many pictures for *Life* and other publications. He says it has often surprised him how many people react personally, and even vehemently, to some feature of a painting. There was a letter he received from a mining town in Canada, whose entire population, of some fifty souls, had taken sides in a dispute over the interpretation of one cover design.

Another time, he drew a picture of a man and a girl kissing— and received a letter, actually threatening in tone, claiming that no man ever kissed a girl that way, and warning Stahr that unless he drew his kisses differently, the writer would come to New York from his distant town and make him change!

THE
ARGOSY™
LIBRARY

GENIUS JONES
BY THE CO-CREATOR OF DOC SAVAGE
LESTER DENT

WHEN TIGERS ARE HUNTING
THE COMPLETE ADVENTURES OF CORDIE, SOLDIER OF FORTUNE, VOLUME 1
W. WIRT

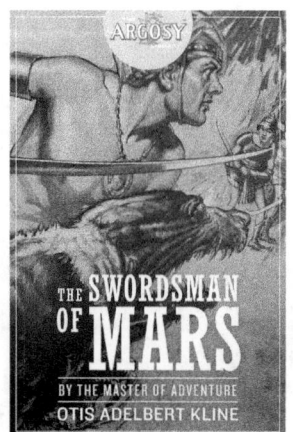

THE SWORDSMAN OF MARS
BY THE MASTER OF ADVENTURE
OTIS ADELBERT KLINE

THE SHERLOCK OF SAGELAND
THE COMPLETE TALES OF SHERIFF HENRY, VOLUME 1
W.C. TUTTLE

GONE NORTH
BY ARGOSY READERS' FAVORITE
CHARLES ALDEN SELTZER

THE MASKED MASTER MIND
BY THE AUTHOR OF PETER THE BRAZEN
GEORGE F. WORTS

BALATA
BY THE AUTHOR OF THE GAMBLER
FRED MacISAAC

BRET-WALDA
BY ARGOSY READERS' FAVORITE
PHILIP KETCHUM

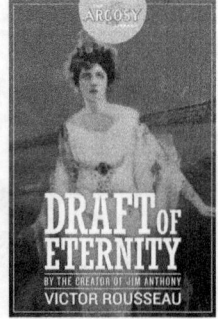

DRAFT OF ETERNITY
BY THE CREATOR OF JIM ANTHONY
VICTOR ROUSSEAU

FOUR CORNERS
VOLUME 1 • BY ARGOSY LEGEND
THEODORE ROSCOE

SERIES 1 • AVAILABLE SPRING 2015